Forgotten Yorkshire Folk and Fairy Tales

Compiled by

Andrew Walsh

Published by Innovative Libraries OU
Sepapaja tn 6, Lasnamäe linnaosa, Tallinn, 15551. Estonia
UK contact: 195 Wakefield Road, Lepton, Huddersfield. HD8 0BL.
andywalsh@innovativelibraries.org.uk
First Published 2019

Text © Copyright Andrew Walsh, 2019

Illustrations © Copyright Jane Carkill, 2019
www.instagram.com/lamblittle

Andrew Walsh asserts his moral rights to be identified as author of this work.
ISBN: 978-1-911500-15-5

Introduction 1

Ainsel 3

All's Well that Ends Well 5

The Barguest (from The Convicts) 13

Auld Betty of Halifax 15

The Banquet of the Dead 17

Billy Biter and Filey Brigg 27

The Boggart 31

The Bosky Dyke Barguest 35

The Building of the Kirk at Heaton 39

The Camblesforth Boggart 43

The Child in the Wood, or the Cruel Uncle 47

Churn Milk Peg 51

The Crafty Ploughboy, or Yorkshire Bite 53

Devil's Bridge 57

The Donkey, the Table, and the Stick 63

The Dragon of Loschy Wood 69

The Drummer Boy of Richmond 73

An Elboton Fairy Dance 75

The Fairies of Willy Houe.......................... 77

The Farndale Hob 79

The Giant of Dalton Mill.......................... 85

The Giant of Sessay 89

The Golden Ball 95

The Golden Cradle and Castle Hill 103

A Grassington Bargest 107

The Hand of Glory.......................... 111

The Hare and the Witch.......................... 119

Janet's Cove 123

A Kilnsay Fairy Dance 131

The Legend of Semerwater 133

Linfit Leadboilers.......................... 137

The Marsden Cuckoo 139

Melch Dick.......................... 141

The Old Woman of Lexhoe 151

Our Lady's Well... 153

The Potato and the Pig.. 155

Potter Thompson 159

The Prophecy 163

The Red Cap of Close House 165

The Return 169

The Serpent of Handale 171

The Seven Sisters & Their Bad Neighbour......... 173

Upsall and its Crocks of Gold 179

Wadda of Mulgrave, and Bell, his Wife. 183

Waffs at the Bridge 187

The White Horse of Wharfedale............................ 189

The Wicked Giant of Penhill 195

The Wise Woman of Littondale............................. 207

A Yorkshire Fairy Reminiscence 217

Key sources & notes 221

v

Introduction

Welcome to this book of Yorkshire folk and fairy tales. It has around fifty tales of dragons, giants, hobs, fairies, witches and other folk, or fairy, tales based in Yorkshire. I've tended to avoid ghost stories, though the odd ghost has sneaked in!

Most of these are unchanged, or with very minor changes, to the versions I've found of them in old (out of copyright) books, though I've tended to soften the dialect to make them easier to read. A few, however, have had slightly more significant changes as the older versions I found were a little brief, and I took a mixture of these and newer versions to retell the story. A couple I've told completely from scratch, building on tiny scraps of local legend, where I could not find a proper story associated with them. There is a list of books at the end, many of which are now freely available online as scanned copies of the originals.

I've pulled these stories together into one place mainly out of frustration at how hard it is to find them otherwise,

As my children (Jennifer & George, now 14 & 13 at the time of writing) were younger, I would have loved to be able to tell them local fairy stories. I looked for them, and found only scraps (for example, 'there is a golden cradle somewhere on Castle Hill') for my local area, Huddersfield. Even looking across the whole of Yorkshire, it was hard to find stories I could tell them.

There is no shortage of adaptions of the Grimm's tales, or Hans Christian Anderson's stories, especially if you want a version heavily flavoured by Disney's treatment of them. But local tales? Not so much…

So here are an assortment of local Yorkshire folk tales and legends. I hope some readers tell and retell them to keep the local stories alive.

Ainsel

A widow and her son, a little boy, lived together in a cottage in or near the village of Rothley. One winter's evening the child refused to go to bed with his mother, as he wished to sit up for a while longer, "*for*," said he, "*I am not sleepy.*" The mother finding remonstrance in vain, at last told him that if he sat up by himself the fairies would most certainly come and take him away.

The boy laughed as his mother went to bed, leaving him sitting by the fire; he had not been there long, watching the fire and enjoying its cheerful warmth, till a beautiful little figure, about the size of a child's doll, descended the chimney and alighted on the hearth!

The little fellow was somewhat startled at first, but its prepossessing smile as it paced to and fro before him soon overcame his fears, and he inquired familiarly, "*What do they ca' thou?*" "*Ainsel,*" answered the little thing haughtily, at the same time retorting the question, *"And what do they ca' thou?"* *"**My** ainsel"* (*my own self*), answered the boy; and they commenced playing together like two children newly acquainted.

Their gambols continued quite innocently until the fire began to grow dim; the boy then took up the poker to stir it, when a hot cinder accidently fell upon the foot of his playmate; her tiny voice was instantly raised to a most terrific roar, and the boy had scarcely time to crouch into the bed behind his mother, before the voice of the fairy's mother was heard shouting, *"Who's done it? Who's done it?"* *"Oh! it was my ainsel!"* answered the daughter. *"Why, then,"* said the mother, as she kicked her up the chimney, *"what's all this noise for: there's nyon (i.e. no one) to blame."*

All's Well that Ends Well

A long time ago, there lived a poor shopkeeper and his family in York, near the Minster. He already had three daughters and two sons, so when his sixth child, another girl, was born he despaired, not knowing how he'd be able to earn enough to feed his family.

"*Alas, woe is me!*" cried the shopkeeper, "*woe is me!*"

As the shopkeeper moaned and cried, a rich and very proud knight, riding past, hear him and called out "*Good man! What ails you so much on this bright and sunny day?*"

"*Oh Sir!*" said the shopkeeper, "*I have six children and I don't know how I will be able to feed them. My youngest was just born, but trade is so bad these days I can't make ends meet.*"

The knight looked into the shop and saw his wife with the new infant. Being well versed in witchcraft, he opened his book of fate to tell the future of the new baby. As soon as he did, he was horrified! He learned that the child, the daughter of a penniless shopkeeper, was destined to marry his own son.

Quickly he closed the book of fate, tried to hide his shock, and smiled at the shopkeeper. He pretended to be keen to adopt the baby, in order to help, bringing her up in a good home where she would want for nothing. The infant was wrapped in a shawl and given to the knight, who rode off with it – not to raise it in a castle, but to throw it straight into the River Ouse.

The baby didn't sink at once, however, and the flow of the river swept it into some reeds. A fisherman saw it, waded across, and rescued the crying infant before it could sink below the water. When he took it home his wife insisted that they keep it, to raise as their own.

Fifteen or sixteen years later, the knight rode that way with a group of friends. He called at the fisherman's cottage to buy something for the cook to prepare for their supper, and the girl answered the door. She pleased him and his friends so much with her conversation that the knight offered to tell her fortune. He opened his book of fate, but imagine his astonishment and anger when it showed him that this was the girl he had thrown into the river as a baby.

Still determined that his son, heir to his fortune and lands, should not marry such a commoner as the shopkeeper's daughter, the knight went on his way, but quickly found an excuse to leave his friends. He returned to the cottage and pretended he had an urgent message that needed to be sent to his brother at Scarborough castle.

The girl, who was as good and kind as she was lovely offered to take the message for him. The knight, thanking her, wrote a letter to his brother, where his son was currently staying too. Then he gave the girl a piece of gold and rode off, chuckling to himself at his cleverness.

The girl set off on her journey, stopping at a wayside inn that night. In the dark, however, a thief broke in to her room and looked through her few belongings for valuables. He opened the letter and read it, learning that the knight had commanded his brother at Scarborough to slay the bearer of the message as soon as she arrived. The thief may not have been a good man, but he couldn't bear to imagine such a young girl tricked and murdered. He wrote another letter, pretending to be from the knight, bidding his brother to arrange the marriage of the girl to the knight's son as soon as was possible. He swapped the letters and left the room without waking the girl.

Two days later, the girl arrived at Scarborough castle and handed over the letter. Once they were introduced, the knight's son was glad to marry her, and within a few days they became man and wife.

Soon after the wedding ceremony, however, the knight arrived. He'd heard the news and furiously angry, had ridden as fast as he could to Scarborough. Realising he was too late to stop the marriage, he dragged the poor girl to the seashore and pulled out his dagger to slay her. The girl begged for her life, and the knight hesitated to kill her. Pulling an unusual ring from his finger, he flung it far out to sea. *"Swear to me that you will never again come within sight of me unless that ring is on your finger,"* he cried, *"and I will spare your life."*

She swore that she would comply, and the knight returned to the castle. The girl began a long and lonely wander up hill and down dale. She did not dare return home, and could do nothing but beg from door to door and do whatever work she could find. One day she knocked on the door of a fine gentleman's house, and was welcomed with kindness. She did such good work running their kitchen that they rewarded her with fine dresses and braid for her hair.

A while later, the gentleman's family invited a number of guests to a feast, which included the knight of York and his son.

The girl wept to see them from the window, as she longed to be back with her husband, but was terrified of being seen by the knight. She did her duty in the kitchen, preparing the meal, including fresh fish that had been delivered that day. As she dressed the fish, she found something glittering inside it, and out came the strange ring that the knight had thrown into the sea months before.

Her sorry turned to joy, and she prepared the meal so well that one of the guests inquired about the cook. A servant was sent to the kitchen so she could be presented to the well fed guests. As soon as she received the summons she washed, dressed in her finest clothes, and entered the banqueting hall.

All the guests turned to look at young girl, except the knight, who immediately drew his sword and rushed towards her. Unafraid, she stood her ground and held her hand in front of her. "*My Lord,*" she said, "*your ring!*"

The knight, finally realising that all his efforts to keep his son and the girl apart were to no avail, sheathed his sword, begged her pardon for all the wrongs he had done to her, and bade her to live in peace and happiness with her son from that day on, which they did.

Most people growing up in Yorkshire will be familiar with a Scarborough warning, where the punishment arrives before you get a chance of doing anything wrong...

> A Scarborough Warning
> A word and a blow
> But the blow first

The Barguest (from The Convicts)

The Barguest is a creature than normally signals that a death is coming, and tends to appear in the form of a large shaggy dog. This is an extract from a work called "The Convicts" describing one!

(extract from New Monthly mag, No. 13., page 65, 1815. "The Convicts")

When darkness o'er the world her mantle throws,
And weary swains have sunk to calm repose,
Except some straggler chance the street to roam,
Who, from the alehouse reeling, seeks his home;
Where late he sate, the blithest of the throng,
None drank more deep, none bawl'd a louder song;
None boasted more of prodigies of might;
Sudden behold him stop, as in affright:
Trembling, he sees before his swimming eyes,
Just in the middle path, a goblin rise,

In form more rugged than Hyrcanian bear,
Whose eyes like burning coals or meteors glare;
A lambent flame plays o'er its rugged hide,
In its own lurid light the demon is descried:
'Tis heard to drag a massy chain behind;
Thick coming fancies fierce assail his mind;
Legends of terror which his grand-dam told,
Now chill the heart of him. of late so bold:
Fast as he flies he hears,
Oh, dire to Close at his heels tell this minister of hell.
Dogs bark, chains rattle, groans and yells resound,
More near they seem'd at every fear-urged bound;
Gasping for joy, he gains his cottage door,
He flies to bed, nor deems himself secure:
Shiv'ring with horror, tells his injur'd wife
The dreadful scene, and vows to mend his life;
Breathes a short prayer, inspir'd alone by fear.

Auld Betty of Halifax

An old man, convinced he had been cursed by Auld Betty the witch, set out on the dangerous task of catching her. She could change her shape, and was often seen in the shape of a black cat.

Sure that she would return to do him harm again, he set a cake baking before the fire and waited, armed and ready with a three-pronged fork. As if out of no-where, a large black cat sat in front of the fire, washing its face, though he hadn't seen or heard it come in.

"*Cake burns*", cried the cat.

"*Turn it then*", replied the man.

"*Cake burns*", cried the cat again.

"*Turn it then*", replied the man.

"*Cake burns*", the cat repeated, and the man made the same answer once more.

The man had been told not to mention any whole name while watching the cat, or to shout, but to instead let the cat become transfixed by the burning cake in the hope it changed shape to stop the cake burning itself. It was late, however, the man was tired, and he lost his temper, swearing at the cat.

Instantly, the cat sprung up the chimney, with the man scrambling after it, trying to pierce it with the three-pronged fork. Although scratched by the cat, he managed this, though the injured cat got away.

The next day auld Betty was ill in her bed, staying there for several days, but the man who had been witched was relieved of all his symptoms.

The Banquet of the Dead

It was the 14th day of July, in the year 1635, when the corpse of a villager was interred in the Churchyard of Kirkby-Malhamdale.

The service finished and all left the churchyard except the sexton, Silas Shaw, a village lad of the name of Kitchen, and a soldier, whose long, flowing, silvery hair and time-worn frame, bespoke a very advanced age. He was seated on a neighbouring stone, from where he raised his eyes to the church and sighed.

Old Silas gazed on the stranger, but didn't recognise him, which meant he couldn't be a local. There was not a nook or corner of the valley, nor of the adjacent one of Otterdale—not a solitary dwelling of which he could not name the dwellers—man, woman, and child. Silas puzzled over him and decided that he'd been a soldier in the King's Army—one of the remnants of Marston Moor, perhaps?

While he pondered, old Silas had been very leisurely pursuing his work. The grave was not yet filled up, and a skull, the remnant of some former occupier of the same narrow cell, was lying beside it. Kitchen took up the skull, and gazed on the sockets. The old soldier observed the boy, and, approaching, said, *"Youth! that belonged to one who died soon after the reign of Queen Mary. His name was Thompson; he was a military man, and as mischievous a fellow as ever existed—aye, for many along year, he was a plague to Malhamdale."*
"Then," replied the boy, *"his death must have been a benefit, the valley must have felt rid of a pest."*

"Why," answered the veteran, *"I fear you are in the wrong. Thompson's reign is not yet finished; 'tis whispered he often returns and revisits his old scenes— nay, even plays his old pranks over again! It is by no means improbable that, at this very instant, he is at no great distance, and listening to our conversation."*

"Indeed!" said Silas; and the sexton rested on his spade, and winked at the soldier; *"that will not*

do! I have been a sexton for many a long year, and I know a trifle or two about ghosts. I often see them, but only after dark. They're like drunkards, fond of late hours. A ghost walking in broad daylight and beneath a broiling July sun! Come, I like that idea well. I wonder where you studied spectre-ology!"

"You hit too hard," said the boy to the sexton; *"I dare say that the old gentlemen there knows more about such than you do. I believe him—but what an old brute this dead man must be! He will neither rest himself nor allow other folks to do so."* Kitchen kicked the skull from him, and remarked, as he heard its hollow sound, *"Well! there's not much there now, whatever there was before!"*

"Boy!" said the soldier, *"you dare not do that again!"*

"Why not?" inquired Kitchen, giving it, at the same time, another hearty kick.

"Kick it again!", said the soldier.

The boy needed no encouragement, and so there was another kick.

The veteran stranger smiled grimly as if pleased with the spirit which the boy showed, and then said, in a joking way, "*Now take up that skull and say to it, let the owner of this meet me at the midnight hour, and invite me to a banquet spread on yon green stone by his bony fingers.*

Come ghost! come devil!
Come good! come evil!
Or let old Thompson himself appear,
For I will partake of his midnight cheer."

Kitchen, laughing with the glee of a schoolboy, repeated the ridiculous invitation, and the no less ridiculous rhymes. He then turned toward the soldier and asked if that would do, or if he had any further requirements, as he should be happy to oblige him; but the warrior was no longer visible.

He had disappeared amidst some lofty limes that then shaded the church-yard. Old Silas had finished his work, and just as the shadow on the dial fell on the hour of twelve, he left the churchyard for the neighbouring inn—the boy at the same time vaulting over the stile that led from the churchyard to the schoolhouse.

Later that day, Kitchen, at his usual hour of ten, retired to rest and soon fell into a deep slumber, from which he was roused by someone rattling the latch and singing beneath the windows. He arose and opened the casement. It was a calm moonlight night, and he distinctly saw the stranger who was rapping at the door and chanting the elegant stanzas which he had dictated at the grave of the villager.

"And, pray, sir, what may you be wanting at this time of night?" asked the boy, wholly undaunted by the strangeness of the visitation. *"If you are not found of going to bed, I am—I can assure you!"*

"'*What*!' replied the stranger, *"Hast thou so soon forgot thy promise?"*, and he repeated the foolish lines.

Kitchen laughed, but the soldier assumed a

peculiar expression. The full gaze of a dark eye, which appeared to glow with something inexpressibly wild and unearthly, was bent upon the boy, who felt a strange sensation steal over his frame, and began to repent of his ill-timed levity.

After a short silence the stranger again addressed him, but in tones so hollow and sepulchral, that his youthful blood was chilled, and his heart beat strongly, and quickly, and audibly.

"Boy! thy word must be kept! Promises made with the grave must not be lightly broken.

Amidst the cold graves of the coffin'd dead,
Is my table deck'd and my banquet spread,
Then haste thee thither, without delay,
Nigh is the time ! — Away! Away"

"Then be it as you wish," said the boy, in some slight degree resuming his courage, *"Go! I will follow!"*

At a short distance from the Church, on the banks of the Aire, was a small cottage, the residence of the Reverend Martin Knowles, the vicar of the parish, who was still sat at his desk preparing a sermon.

He jumped as the quiet was broken by a hurried and violent knocking at the door. It was Kitchen with a face as pale as a winding sheet.

"*Kitchen!*" said the minister, "*what brings you here at this untimely hour?*" He gave a somewhat confused and rushed account of everything that happened, and asked for the minister's help.

The minister and the lad proceeded towards the churchyard. The minister looked around, but no one was visible at first, until a dark shadowy form appeared, slowly gliding amidst the tombstones.

It approached, and, as it came closer, the minister recognised the mysterious being described by the terrified boy.

"*The figure stopped and said, 'One! Two! How is this? I have one more guest than I expected, but it matters not—all is ready, follow!*

> *'Amidst the cold graves of the coffin'd dead,*
> *Is my table deck'd and my banquet spread,*
> *Haste ye thither without delay,*
> *Now is the time!—Away! Away!"*

The figure waved its arm impatiently, and, beckoning them to follow, moved on in the precise and measured step of an old soldier. Having reached the altar window, it turned towards a corner of the building and proceeded directly to an old green stone.

Upon it a feast was prepared. The stone was plentifully bedecked; yet it was an awful sight to see, where, till now, none but the earth-worm had ever revelled, a banquet prepared as for revelry. The boy looked on the smoking viands, and a strange thought crossed his mind. At what fire were those provisions cooked? The seats were coffins, and Kitchen every instant seemed to dread lest the owners should appear and join in the sepulchral banquet. Their ghostly host having placed himself at the head of the table, he motioned his guests to do the same.

The minister, who was rather an epicure, glanced his eyes over the stone, and finding that necessary accompaniment to a good supper, salt, was missing, exclaimed in an astonished tone, "*Why, where's the salt?*" when immediately the stranger and his feast vanished, and of all that banquet nothing remained, save the mossy stone whereon it had been spread.

There is a circular pit near Flamborough where a girl named Jenny Gallows is supposed to have committed suicide. If you run nine times around this pit, you'll be able to hear the fairies. There is a risk though... when you have gone eight times around, the spirit of Jenny, all clothed in white, rises from the water and says:

> Ah'll tee on me bonnet
> An' put on me shoe,
> An' if thoo's not off
> Ah'll suan catch thoo!

Billy Biter and Filey Brigg

A couple of hundred years ago, a huge dragon, nearly a mile long, lived in the waters near Filey. It had a habit of lying in the gulley, a tidal inlet, where it was partly hidden, and making itself a snack of any unsuspecting boats that ventured near.

Ralph Parkin, known as Billy Biter to his friends, for reasons too obscure to go into here, lived in Filey all his life, working as a tailor in the town. One day, he went down to the beach for a breath of fresh air and to eat some of the cake his wife had made him.

The dragon was getting restless, however, and its nostrils flared as the smell of the cake drifted over from Billy's hand. It was the sticky gingerbread style cake made in Yorkshire from plenty of oatmeal and treacle, and it made the serpent's stomach growl with hunger.

It heaved its huge bulk up from the water

and scared poor Billy half to death. In a panic, he threw the whole cake at the dragon, who chomped down in satisfaction. It was too sticky and rich for the dragon, however, who was used to crunchier and meatier snacks, and its teeth got stuck together. It thrashed around in the water, trying to unstick its jaws, repeatedly dunking its head in the water to wash the cake away.

Billy saw his chance, and jumped onto the dragon's head while it was just under the surface of the water. He called to his friends to do the same, and their combined weight drowned the dragon.

To this day, the sticky ginger cake is known as Parkin after the family who made the cake that killed the Filey dragon. The bones of the great serpent still lie where he died, jutting out to sea, and are known as Filey Brigg.

Incidentally, after the dragon died, the devil took to hunting for drowned souls in Filey Bay. He'd stand next to the Brigg and smash holes in the bottoms of ships as they passed. One day he dropped his hammer in the bay. Reaching around under the water for it, he grabbed a haddock by mistake, and that is why haddocks still have black thumb prints on their shoulders today.

Hob rhyme (1):

Hob-hole Hob!

Mah Bairn's getten t'kin-cough,

Tak't off, tak't off.

The Boggart

(from The London literary gazette and journal of belles lettres, arts, sciences, etc., 1825, no. 430, page 252,253.)

One day, a Boggart took up residence (why and how, I never discovered) in the house of a quiet, inoffensive farmer, George Gilbertson.

Once there, it seemed to decide that it was the rightful owner and caused a good deal of annoyance. They never saw it of course, as a Boggart is rarely visible to the human eye, though it is frequently seen by cattle and horses. (A Yorkshire term for a 'shying horse' is one that has 'taken the boggle'.)

It seemed to take a particular dislike to the children, tormenting them in various ways. Sometimes their bread and butter would be snatched away, or their porringers of bread and milk be capsized by an invisible hand; at other times, the curtains of their beds would be shaken backwards and forwards, or a heavy weight would press on and nearly suffocate them. The parents had often, on hearing their cries, to fly to their aid.

There was a kind of closet, formed by a wooden partition on the kitchen-stairs, and a large knot having been driven out of one of the deal-boards of which it was made, there remained a hole. Into this one day the farmer's youngest boy stuck the shoe-horn with which he was amusing himself, when immediately it was thrown out again, and struck the boy on the head. The agent was of course the Boggart, and though the first time was terrifying, it soon became their amusement (which they called laikin' wi' Boggart) to put the shoe-horn into the hole and have it shot back at them. This seemed to goad the Boggart into more disruptive behaviour.

At night, heavy steps were heard clattering down the stairs, like someone wearing clogs. Sounds like earthernware and pewter dishes smashing against the kitchen floor were heard, though the dishes were intact on their shelves in the morning.

    The Boggart at length proved such a torment that the farmer and his wife resolved to quit the house and let him have it all to himself. This was put into execution, and the farmer and his family were following the last loads of furniture, when a neighbour named John Marshall came up—"*Well, Georgey,*" said he, "*and soa you're leaving t'ould hoose at last?*"—"*Heigh, Johnny, my lad, I'm forced tull it; for that damned Boggart torments us soa, we can neither rest neet nor day for't. It seems loike to have such a malice again t'poor bairns, it o'most kills my poor dame here at thoughts on't, and soa, ye see, we're forced to flitt loike.*" He scarce had uttered the words when a voice from a deep upright churn cried out, "*Aye, aye, Georgey, we're flitting ye see.*"—"*'Od damn thee,*" cried the poor farmer, "*if I'd known thou'd been there, I wadn't ha' stirred a peg. Nay, nay, it's no use, Mally,*" turning to his wife, "*we *may as weel turn back again to t'ould hoose as be tormented in another that's not so convenient."*

I believe they did turn back, and seemed to come to a better understanding with the Boggart, though it continued its trick of firing the horn from the knot-hole. I remember an old tailor, who used to visit the farmhouse on his rounds, told me the horn was frequently pitched at his head, many years after this first took place.

The Bosky Dyke Barguest

Near Fewston, in the Forest of Knaresborough, is a spot named Busky or Bosky Dike — no doubt from the bushes, locally called busks or bosks, with which the sides of the narrow gill, through which the brook or dyke runs, were at one time covered. It was regularly haunted by a Barguest, who tended to disappear in the same spot, where a large drain crosses the road. It hasn't been seen since a school was built there in 1878.

The Bosky Dyke, the Bosky Dyke,
Ah ! tread its path with care;
With silent step haste through its shade,
For 'Bargest' wanders there!

Since days when ev'ry wood and hill
By Pan or Bel was crowned;
And ev'ry river, brook, and copse
Some heathen goddess owned.

Since bright the Druid's altar blazed,
And lurid shadows shed,
On Almus Cliff and Brandrith Rocks,
Where human victims bled.

Hag-witches oft, 'neath Bestham oaks,
Have secret revels kept,
And fairies danced in Clifton Field,
When men unconscious slept.

Dark sprite and ghost of every form,
No man e'er saw the like,
Have played their pranks at midnight hours,
In haunted Busky Dyke.

There milk-white cats, with eyes of fire,
Have guarded stile and gate,
And calves and dogs of wondrous shape,
Have met the trav'ller late.

And 'Pad-foot' oft, in shaggy dress,
With many a clanking chain,
Before the astonished rustic's eyes,
Has vanished in the drain.

On winter's eve, by bright wood fire,
As winter winds do roar,
And heap the snow on casement higher,
Or beat against the door.

Long tales are told from sire to son,
In many a forest ingle,
Of rushing sounds and fearful sights,
In Busky Dyke's dark dingle.

But lo! there now, as deftly reared,
As if by magic wands,
In superstition's own domain,
A village schoolroom stands.

Where thickest fell the gloom of night,
And terror held its sway,
Now beams the rising sun of light,
And intellectual day.

Before its beams, its warmth, its power,
Let every phantom melt,
And children's gambols now be heard,
Where fearful bargest dwelt.

Yet softly tread, with rev'rent step.
Along the Busky shade,
There ghosts our fathers feared of old.
Will be for ever laid.

The Building of the Kirk at Heaton

I've often wondered why the church (or Kirk) was built where it was in Kirkheaton. It sits at the edge of the village, next to the pub (or the Kirk Stile) built to keep the churchmen well lubricated between services, but well away from the old village centre.

Some say that it was never meant to be there, but instead was intended for a site nearer the centre of the village. The old wooden church had stood there until around 1200AD, and the locals were proud to be starting to build a stone church in its place.

They cleared the land ready, the first few carts of stone were delivered, and the masons started to build up the walls. The locals looked on with pride, knowing that they'd be building a church that could last many centuries into the future.

While this was going on, the devil watched

unseen, and decided to play a trick on these proud villagers.

After the first week of building, and once the workmen had left for the night, the devil spirited away all the stones and the half built walls and placed them half a mile away at the bottom of the village.

Waking up the next day, they were shocked to see all their hard work not only gone, but rebuilt half a mile away! After much cursing and confusion, they demolished the part built walls and moved the stone back to the desired site. A week later, after working harder than before, they started to feel they'd got back to the stage they'd been in before – the walls were part built and going up well, they were getting into a rhythm with the building, and were starting to wonder if they still needed to set a watchman overnight to keep an eye on the building.

That was when the devil struck again. The watchman claimed he only blinked for a moment and the church had gone! Once more, they found it moved down the hill and rebuilt in the wrong place.

Once more, they laboriously moved the stones back up the hill and started again. This repeated itself just a few days later!

This third time, they had had enough, and just carried on building in the 'wrong' place. The devil had his fun, and the village gained its church… just in a different place than first planned.

An old children's rhyme. In Norse mythology Nanna was a moon goddess, wife of Baldur. So a rhyme to celebrate a full moon perhaps?

> The moon shines bright,
> The stars give light,
> And little Nanny Button-cap
> Will come tomorrow night.

The Camblesforth Boggart

This is a story only minimally tweaked from a report in The Huddersfield Chronicle and West Yorkshire Advertiser (West Yorkshire, England), Saturday, February 25, 1860; pg. 3; Issue 519. British Library Newspapers, part II: 1800-1900.

In 1860, a newspaper reported an incident in the farm-house and premises of Mr Thomas Duckles and his wife, both of whom were over 80.

They had suffered from some mysterious and troublesome happenings, with a large cast iron kitchen fender (weighing 5 or 6 stones) jumping from one room to another, their fire irons dancing around the house as though doing a jig at an Irish wedding, and their iron hatchet boldly splitting the outhouse door in an attempt to join the other ironmongery in their dance. The poor couple announced they were unable to stay in the house, with such chaos taking place.

Several of their neighbours investigated, and many a valiant man bore testimony to the abuse they suffered on entering the house. A pot of lamp-black blinded one man, and a large hamper extinguished another while he descended the farmhouse stairs. These stories are so numerous, that a whole newspaper may be filled with the stories, with people coming from Selby, Snaith, Rawcliffe, Carlton, and all the neighbouring towns and villages to an incredible distance. This adventure has been seen as so perilous that many armed themselves with weapons such as double-barrelled guns, revolvers, pikes, and other warlike weapons indescribable to those of a delicate disposition.

The district wise man has been consulted, the police force requisitioned, and the most active measures possible taken for four or five nights in succession to try to discover the hidden cause of these outrages.

An innocent Scotswoman has been accused of witchcraft by the old women of the district, and a thousand and one influences have been attributed to the living and dead of bygone ages.

Whether the cause of these disturbances are natural, or a result of magic or the black arts, has yet to be discovered. The ingenuity of the locals, the parochial authorities, and the civil powers being entirely insufficient, an assembly of local clergy was observed discussing the mysteries of Camblesforth Grange. Even the landlord of Mr Duckles, the gallant Colonel Thompson, got involved, but no-one ever discovered the true cause and the mystery of the Camblesforth Boggart remains.

A witch's curse:

Fire cum,

Fire Gan,

Curlin' smeak,

Keep oo o' t'pan;

Ther's a teead i' t'fire, a frog on t'hob,

Here's t'heart frev a crimson ask,

Here's a teeath fra t'heead

O' yan a's deead,

At nivver gat thruff his task;

Here's prick'd I' blood a maiden's prayer,

At t'e e o' maunt see,

It's prick'd upon a yet warm mask,

An' lapt aboot a breet green ask,

An' it's all fer him and thee.

It boils,

Thoo'll drink,

He'll speak,

Thoo'll think,

It boils,

Thoo'll see,

He'll speak,

Thoo'll dee.

The Child in the Wood, or the Cruel Uncle

In the town on Beverley, in Yorkshire, about 2 years ago (1703), there lived a squire called Somers, who was a very honest gentleman with a good income. He lived with his wife and two year old daughter. Unfortunately, after a short illness, his wife died, leaving him heartbroken. He found he couldn't enjoy life at all after his loss, and soon fell ill, took to his bed and died after just a fortnight of illness himself.

While ill, he sent for his brother, who lived about 14 miles away, and begged him to take care of his daughter in case he didn't recover. "*Brother*", he said, "*I leave with you the dearest thing that I have in the world, my little daughter. Together with her, I entrust my whole estate. Manage it for her use, and take care of her education and upbringing. Look after her as if she was your own, and for my sake, see her married to an honest country gentleman.*" His brother faithfully promised to do this should he not

47

recover, so when the gentleman died, the brother takes the little girl home and looked after her kindly for some time.

But it didn't take long before he became jealous of the fortune that he was looking after for her. He plotted many different ways in which he could take the estate for himself, and eventually decided to abandon her in the woods. He couldn't bring himself to murder her outright, so took her to a hollow tree, gagged her mouth so she couldn't be heard crying, and left her inside the hollow. To conceal the crime, he had commissioned a wax model of a child to be made. Once the child was abandoned in the hollow tree, he dressed the wax effigy in a shroud, laid it in a coffin, and held a great funeral for the girl. The wax model was buried, and no one suspected anything but an illness and a sad, young death, all too common in young children.

At the same time this was happening, a neighbouring gentleman dreamed that the following day he would see something that would astonish him. He told it to his wife, who tried to persuade him to stay at home, but he took no notice and went out hunting instead. As he rode through the woods that morning, his horse was startled and nearly knocked him from his saddle. He turned around, looking for what had disturbed his horse, and saw something move in a dark hole. Worried now that his dream was coming true, he told one of his servants to check the hole - it was the same hollow in a tree that the little girl had been abandoned in, and they pulled her out, barely still alive.

He took her home, looking after her as her strength returned, but she was too young to be able to tell them where she had come from. This remained a mystery until Christmas, and they held a feast and a singing at his house. One of his guests recognised the little girl and told them she was supposedly dead and buried. Shocked, the gentleman went to the parish minister and persuaded him to have the grave dug up, discovering the wax model inside the coffin.

The cruel Uncle was arrested and convicted of abandoning the child and attempting to steal her inheritance, and the court decided that the gentleman who found her should be allowed to look after her as if she was his own. This pleased him and his wife greatly, as they had no other children, and had already grown fond of the little girl, looking after her from then onwards as if she was their own.

Churn Milk Peg

The road called Short Lea Lane is linked with fairy lore, being a favourite haunt of Churn-milk Peg, a being, perhaps, peculiar to Craven.

Peg is represented as an old and very ugly hag, with a pipe in her mouth. Her job is to protect the nuts, when in the pulpy state called churn-milk, from being gathered by naughty children. All she says is:

'Smoke! Smoke a wooden pipe!
Getting nuts before they're ripe!"

If this rhyme does not succeed in scaring the children, then churn-milk Peg 'tacks em!' This creature is known in Malhamdale, where fruit-pilfering children are told to *"tak care, or Churn-milk Peg will tak ye to t'owd lad*!", the old lad being the devil perhaps?

A protective charm. It sounds like this must work when it is tied around your neck as the source says: "I have tried this for many years and no evil came nigh my flocks, save when the charmed one strayed from the flock", which sounds like a recommendation to me...

> Tak' twea at's red an' yan at's black
> O' poison berries three,
> Three fresh-cull'd blooms o' Devil's glut,
> An a sprig o' rosemary;
> Tak henbane, bullace, bumm'lkite,
> An' t'fluff frev a deead bulrush,
> Nahn berries shak' fra t'rowan tree,
> An' nahn fra bottery bush.

The Crafty Ploughboy, or Yorkshire Bite

One morning, George, the farmer's labourer, was called in to the farmhouse.

'Now then George', the farmer said, *'I want you to take this cow to the fair. We don't need her, but she's a good 'un, so we can spare her for sale. Make sure you get a good price for her mind.'*

So George took her off to the fair and found a couple of men in need of expanding their herd. He haggled well, and got a good price for her.

Pleased with his morning's work, he stopped for a quick drink and a bite to eat before he returned to the farm. The money lay heavy in his pocket and he was a little worried about how to keep it safe on the way back. Talking to the landlady of the inn, she suggested sewing it in the lining of his coat, so no-one would now it was there.

'A great idea', he replied. *'I'll sew this money into the lining of my coat before I leave this inn!'*

Unfortunately, a highwayman was listening to their conversation. He sat there watching him hiding the money and followed George when he left.

Once the highwayman saw which direction young George was walking, he gave him a few minutes head start. He then got his horse ready and made sure he rode just fast enough to catch up with him.

'Hello there', the highwayman called. *'These roads are dangerous and two can travel more safely than one. If I offer you a lift behind me on my horse, would you keep me company for safety?'*

George agreed, thankful to have a lift instead of having to walk the full way home. They rode on for a couple of miles, until they were well out of sight and hearing of anyone else, along a dark, sheltered lane. This is when the highwayman drew his pistol and revealed his plan, threatening to kill George unless he handed over the money.

So George jumped straight down off the horse and tore the lining of his coat open so that the money spilled on the ground.

'Take it', George cried. *'I'll not argue with an armed man!'*.

The highwayman instantly knelt down and started to pick the money up from amongst the long grass at the side of the lane. George was no fool, however, and seized his chance, jumping back onto the horse and riding away before the highwayman could stand and take aim at him.

Returning to the farm, George's master was amazed to see him riding up the lane.

'What on earth has happened?', he cried. *'Has my cow turned into a horse?'*

George replied that though he had sold the cow for a fair price, he'd lost the money to a highwayman. To make amends, he'd brought home his horse, saddle and bridle instead.

His master laughed out loud, and carried on laughing as they opened the saddlebags and found two hundred pounds in silver and gold, with two pairs of pistols.

'You've been very bold, young George', laughed the farmer. *'As for the villain it serves him right. You've put upon him, a true Yorkshire bite.'*

'That's true', replied George. *'I think I sold your cow well today.'*

So George, for his bravery and quick thinking, got three quarters of the money for his share, and the highwayman got an expensive lesson in trying to part a Yorkshireman from his money.

Devil's Bridge

The highway between Pateley Bridge and Grassington crosses, in the parish of Burnsall, the deep dell in which runs the small river Dibb, or Dibble, by a bridge known in legend as the Devil's Bridge. It might reasonably be supposed that Deep -dell Bridge, or Dibble Bridge, was the correct and desirable designation, but legend and local tradition will by no means have it so, and account for the less pleasant name in the following manner.

In the days when Fountain's Abbey was in its prime, a shoemaker and small tenant of part of the Abbeylands, named Ralph Calvert, resided at Thorp-sub-Montem, and journeyed twice a year along this road to pay his rent to the Abbot, dispose of the fruits of his six months' handiwork, and return the shoes entrusted to him on his previous visit for repair, and bring back with him, on his return, a bag well filled with others that needed his attention.

The night before setting out, on one of these occasions, he had a fearful dream, in which he struggled with the devil, who, in this wild, rocky ravine, amid unpleasant surroundings, endeavoured to thrust Ralph into a bag, similar to the one in which he carried his stock-in-trade. This he and his wife feared boded no good. In the morning, however, he started on his journey, and duly reached the abbey, assisted at the service, did his business with the abbot and brethren, and then started, with his well-filled bag, on his return homewards. When he arrived near home, in the deep ravine, where on previous occasions he had found but a small brook which he could easily ford, he now found a mountain torrent, through which he only with difficulty and some danger made his way. Having accomplished the passage, he sat down to rest and to dry his wetted garments. As he sat and contemplated the place, he could not but recall how exactly it corresponded with the spot seen in his dream, and at which the author of evil had tried to bag him. Dwelling on this brought anything but pleasant thoughts, and to drive them away, and to divert his mind, he struck up a familiar song, in which the name of the enemy finds frequent mention, and the refrain of which was:

"Sing luck-a-down heigh down,

Ho, down derry"

He was unaware of any presence but his own; but, to his alarm another voice than his added a further line:

"Tol lol derol, darel del, dolde deny."

Ralph thought of his dream. Then he fancied he saw the shadow of a man on the road; then from a projecting comer of a rock he heard a voice reading over a list of delinquents in the neighbourhood, with whom he must remonstrate— Ralph's own name among the rest.

Not to be caught eavesdropping Ralph feigned sleep; but after a time was aroused by the stranger, and a long conversation ensued, the upshot of which was, after they had entered into a compact of friendship, that Satan informed the shoemaker who he was, and inquired of the alarmed man if there was anything that he could do for him.

Ralph looked at the swollen torrent, and thought of the danger he had lately incurred in crossing it, and of his future journeys that way to the abbey; and then he said, "*I have heard that you are an able architect; I should wish you to build a bridge across this stream; I know you can do it.*"

"*Yes*", replied his visitant, "*I can and will do it. At the fourth day from this time, come to this spot and you will be astonished, and you can bring the whole countryside with you, if you like.*"

At nightfall Ralph reached his home at Thorpe, and related his adventure to his wife, and added, "*In spite of all that is said against him, the Evil One is an honest gentleman, and I have made him promise to build a bridge at the Gill Ford on the road to*

Pateley. If he fulfils his promise, St. Crispin bless him."

The news of Ralph's adventure and of the promise soon spread among the neighbours, and he had no small amount of village chaff and ridicule to meet before the eventful Saturday — the fourth day — arrived. At last it came. Accompanied by thirty or forty of the villagers, Ralph made his way to the dell, where, on arrival, picture their astonishment at the sight! Lo, a beautiful and substantial bridge spanned the abyss. A surveyor, and mason, and priest pronounced it to be perfect.

The latter sprinkled it with holy water, caused a cross to be placed at each approach to it, and then declared it to be safe for all Christian people to use. So it remained until the Puritan Minister of Pateley, in the time of the Commonwealth, discerning the story to be a Popish legend, caused the protecting crosses to be removed as idolatrous.

After that time, neither the original builder, nor any other person, seems to have thought fit to keep the bridge in "good and tenantable" repair, and in time it fell into so disreputable and dangerous a condition, that the liberal, and almost magic-working, native of the parish — Sir William Craven, Lord Mayor of London in the reign of the first James — took the matter in hand, and built upon the old foundations a more terrestrial, but not less substantial and enduring, structure.

Still men call it the Devil's Bridge.

The Donkey, the Table, and the Stick

A Lepton lad called George was once so desperate to leave home, that he decided to run away and to seek his fortune on his own.

He ran off down the lane, through the woods, up the hill, and onwards until he bumped into an old women collecting sticks for her fire. He apologised as best he could, for he was still puffing and panting from his long run, but the woman laughed it off as George picked up the sticks now scattered around them.

'You look like a good lad', she said.*' Would you like to work for me? I'll see you'll be paid well, don't you fear'.* George was hungry and a little worried about where he would sleep that night anyway, so he agreed.

He served the woman for a year and a day, to the best of his abilities. The woman called him in, saying *'You've worked well, time for your wages'*. She presented him with a donkey and told him that whenever he was short of money, all he needed to do was pull his ears. George gave it a go, and as the donkey brayed, out dropped silver and gold coins.

He was pleased his labour had earned him such a prize, and he rode away on the donkey until he reached an Inn. Walking in, he ordered the best food and drink, and their best bed for the night. Well, the Innkeeper refused to believe such a young lad had coins to spare to pay, so he demanded payment up front. So, the boy went into the stable, pulled the donkey's ears and collected a pocketful of money. The Innkeeper had secretly watched this and while George slept, he switched the donkey with one of his own.

George was none the wiser the next morning, and set off again towards his old home. As he arrived, he walked in saying all their money worries were over and pulled the donkey's ears. Of course, it brayed away like a good 'un, but no coins came out! Ashamed, he ran away again.

He ran, and he ran, until he could run no more, this time stopping at a weaver's place. *'You look a good lad',* said the weaver, *'serve me and I'll make sure you're paid well, don't you fear'*. So took another risk, and worked for the joiner. After another year and a day, the joiner called him in for his wages. He passed George a tablecloth and told him to cover the table with it, then say the words '*Table be covered*'. He did, and at once a great feast of food and drink appeared on the table.

George was pleased with this, thinking he and his family need never go hungry again. So his folded it up, and set off home. Again, he stopped off at the same Inn. *'Innkeeper'*, he shouted, *'what is there to eat tonight?'*.

'Nothing but oatcakes and week-long stew', the Innkeeper replied.

So George pulled out his tablecloth, said the magic phrase, and produced a marvellous feast. The Innkeeper was amazed, but said nothing.

That night, while George slept, the Innkeeper swapped the amazing tablecloth with an old one of his own.

George was none the wiser the next morning, and set off again towards his old home. As he arrived, he told his family that they would never go hungry again and produced the tablecloth. *'Table be covered'*, said George, but of course nothing happened. So, even more embarrassed than last time, but convinced now that something had happened at the Inn, George ran off again.

He ran and ran, not paying attention to where he went, and fell into the river! A man pulled him out and asked George to help him in exchange – he wanted to make a bridge across the river from one of the trees on the bank.

Well, climbing trees was one of George's favourite pastimes as a lad, so he climbed straight to the top of one. He swayed back and forth on the tree, while the man chopped at the roots, until the whole tree toppled over. A little trimming of branches and it made a fine bridge to walk across the river.

The man thanked him, fettled one of the side branches into a club, and offered it to George as payment for his help. *'Say to the stick, 'Up stick and bang him', and it will knock down anyone who angers you'*, instructed the man.

George went straight to the Inn with his new stick, and as soon as the Innkeeper appeared, called *'Up stick and bang him'*. The club beat the Innkeeper on the back and legs until he fell to the floor and confessed everything to George, if only he would make the stick stop.

The donkey and tablecloth now returned to him, George set off proudly towards his old home. He laid a feast on the table, and pulled the donkey's ears until he had a chest full of gold.

It soon got around Lepton that George had returned with a fortune, and all the local girls set their caps at him. He let it be known that he would marry the richest lass in town, and asked them all to come to the house with their money in their aprons.

All the girls lined up the next morning, with gold and silver in their aprons, but his childhood sweetheart had only a few coppers. He told her to stand to one side, but as tears ran down her cheeks, they turned to diamonds as they hit her apron.

'Up stick and bang them', George shouted, and the remaining girls were beaten until they ran out of sight. George picked up the money they'd dropped as they ran away and poured it into his childhood sweetheart's apron. *'Now you are the richest lass in town, with diamonds, gold and silver, and I shall marry thee'*.

The Dragon of Loschy Wood

In the church of Nunnington, in North Yorkshire, is an ancient tomb. It is topped by the figure of a knight in armour, lying prone, the legs crossed, the feet resting against a dog, the hands apparently clasping a heart, but no inscription to determine to whom the monument belongs.

The locals tell that it is the tomb of Peter Loschy, a famous warrior, whose last exploit was killing a huge serpent, or dragon, which infested the country, and had its den on a wooded landmark now called Loschy Hill.

They say that having determined to free the area from the pest, Peter Loschy asked why no-one else had yet succeeded in destroying the serpent. Even the strongest and bravest warriors had failed, as it seemed able to recover from any wound inflicted upon it, shaking off a strike from a sword like we would a bite from a gnat.

Peter, therefore, made extra plans, getting a suit of armour prepared, with every part of it being covered with razor-blades set with the edges pointing outwards. Thus defended, armed with his sword, and accompanied by a faithful dog, he went forth to seek the dragon, which he quickly found in a thicket on the Hill.

The dragon, glad of another victim, pounced upon the armed man, ignoring a wound from Peter's sword, and folded itself around his body, intending to squeeze Peter to death, and afterwards to devour him at leisure, but in this it was disappointed.

The razor-blades were sharp, and pierced it all over, so it quickly uncoiled itself again. To the surprise of the knight, as soon as it pulled away from him and the razor blade coated armour, its wounds instantly healed, and it was strong and vigorous as ever.

A long and desperate fight ensued between the knight and the serpent, without either gaining much advantage over the other.

With Peter tiring, and fearing he could never inflict a fatal injury on the serpent, his swung his sword once more and chopped a segment from the end of the dragon's tail.

His faithful dog saw his chance and quickly snatched up the beast's flesh and ran across the valley with it for nearly a mile. He left it on a hill near Nunnington Church, and immediately returned to the scene of combat. Snatching up another fragment, he took it to the same place, and returned again and again for other fragments until they were all removed, the last portion taken being the poisonous head.

The knight, now rejoicing at his victory, stooped to pat and praise his faithful dog, who looked up and licked the knight's face. Sadly, the poison of the serpent was still on the dog's tongue, and both fell down dead within an hour of their victory.

The villagers buried the body of the knight in Nunnington Church, and placed a monument over the grave, on which were carved the figures of the knight and his faithful dog, to witness to the truth of the story.

The Drummer Boy of Richmond

There were legends that tunnels ran under the countryside near Richmond Castle, but no-one knew where the entrances were. That is, until a group of soldiers, stationed nearby, found what looked like a tunnel entrance while on patrol in the area.

The entrance was tiny though, and none of the soldiers could squeeze through. Rather than trying to dig it out, they sent for the Regimental Drummer Boy instead. They gave him a lantern, his drum, and helped him wiggle through the tiny entrance.

Once in, he played his drum as he moved along the tunnel, with the soldiers following the sound of the drum from above ground. It worked for a while, and the soldiers followed the drumming towards the abbey, which used to have close links with the Norman castle.

Suddenly, however, the sound of the

drumming changed, as the drummer boy had entered a large chamber. A large group of knights were in an enchanted sleep, along with King Arthur and his mighty sword Excalibur. A knight raised his hand to silence the load drumming, and above ground the soldiers heard instead the faint whispers of a conversation taking place.

'Is England in danger?', the knight asked. *'No'*, the boy replied. *'Then now is not the time to awaken King Arthur'*, said the knight. *'Will you stay with us, and sleep until we are needed?'*. In great excitement and pride, the boy agreed, and still lies there to this day.

An Elboton Fairy Dance

An inhabitant of a village, not far from Elboton, was passing the mountain on a moonlight night, when he saw the fairies dancing.

He knew their laws and regulations, but having taken too much "rum and water" at a neighbouring public house he so far forgot himself as to volunteer a song (some say it was

"*Tarry Woo* ") and he joined the festive circle without being invited. He was punished by kicks and pinches; and so was obliged to make a hasty departure.

However, as he was being driven away, he avenged himself by taking one of the fairies prisoner, and putting it safe and sound into his pocket.

When he got to his home he was sobered with the effects of his adventure, and his children were delighted to hear of the capture of a living doll.

But alas! The fairy had managed to escape; and to make matters worse, the affair, when mentioned to others, was regarded as either an invention or a drunken dream!

The Fairies of Willy Houe

Among the ancient grave-mounds, or barrows, in the Wold districts of Yorkshire, which were favourite haunts of the fairies, no place was more favoured by them than "Willy Houe", a large barrow near Wold Newton in the East Riding.

It is related of this spot, by William of Newborough, an Augustinian canon, whose chronicle terminates about the time of the death of Richard I., that as a man was riding, late at night, near Willy Houe, he heard the most soft and delightful music proceeding from it. He carefully approached the place, and then saw, through a door open in the side of the mound, a magnificent hall, with a great company of fairies banqueting therein. Before he could withdraw, an attendant came forth and offered to him drink, from a magnificent cup. He knew the danger of eating, or drinking, with fairies, and resisted the temptation, but seized the cup from the hand of the cup-bearer and succeeded, though hotly pursued by the whole company, in carrying it off in safety. "It was", says the chronicler, "a vessel of unknown material, of unusual colour and shape".

The legend as told in the locality now, states that it was of fairy gold, and so of no value. It was given to Henry I., who seems to have thought it of sufficient value, intrinsic or otherwise, to send to his brother-in-law, David, King of Scotland, to whom, it is said, he presented it.

The Farndale Hob

In days past, when fairy folk were more commonly found than today, a farmer called Jennifer lived in Farndale with her husband.

One night she was fast asleep in her bed, when a thumping sound woke her. At first she felt she must be dreaming, but the thumping continued, and she became convinced it was coming from the barn.

The whole family gathered downstairs, unsure what to do, but there was such a racket coming from the barn, no-one dared investigate. Instead they made sure the doors were all locked securely and waited until the morning, so they could check in daylight.

Dawn broke, and the family cautiously opened the doors. Jennifer tiptoed up to the barn and carefully peered through a crack in the door. She was amazed at what she saw! The thumping noise must have been corn being threshed. In one night, more corn had been threshed than they could have done in a week.

The next night the noise started again, but they felt a little safer after seeing what had happened the night before and slept a little better too. By the morning, all the corn they'd harvested had been threshed.

The helper returned again a while later, shearing all the sheep in one night the next summer, and mowing the hay another time. The family got used this, and felt thankful that a hob had moved in to offer his unseen help. They didn't know how to show their thanks, however, as hobs and fairies can be a tad funny in their dealings with people, especially if offered clothes to wear.

So they tried leaving a bowl of cream out at night for the hob, as a treat to show him how much they appreciated him. Sure enough, the cream was gone the next morning and the bowl was clean. For the price of a bowl of cream each night, Jennifer and her farm had gained the best farm worker they'd ever had.

The good times didn't last forever though. One winter, her husband became sick of the fever and died. She remarried after a while, but her new husband was a mean and jealous man. He resented the best cream being left out for the hob each night and told her she was wasting it on cats and rats who would be helping themselves to it each night.

One day, Jennifer knew she'd be working late, so asked her new husband to put the cream out for the hob in case she didn't return in time. Instead of the cream, however, he put out the thin whey left over cheesemaking instead.

For the first time in years, the farm was silent that night. No corn was threshed, no sheep sheared, no spinning done. There was to be no help any night from then on. Instead, everything started to go wrong on the farm. The butter wouldn't churn, the cheese went black with mould, and foxes killed the chickens. Every week, there were new disasters on the farm, and they struggled to make ends meet.

Strange noises and screams were heard at night, and things moved mysteriously around the farm, scaring the rest of the farm workers away. Gates were left open, allowing animals to wander off, and candles blew out at the darkest point of night.

With the farm going to rack and ruin, Jennifer decided they must move on and leave the angry hob behind. They loaded all their possessions onto a cart and said goodbye to the farm.

As they road along the lane, one of their neighbours came out to see what was happening.

"How do, Jennifer. Has it really come to this?", he asked.

"Aye, George", she replied. *"It really has come to it, we're flitting"*.

At that point they heard another voice…

"Aye, we've flitting."

Sat on top of their cart was the strangest, hairiest little creature you've ever seen. He chuckled as they turned to him.

Jennifer knew she was beaten and turned the cart around to head back to the farm. *"We were flitting, but if you're flitting with us we may as well flit back. For I see now that for us there is no hope."*

Sad to say, she was right. So if you hear strange noises in the night and think you may have a hob living with you, make sure you reward it well and don't annoy him, otherwise, you'll always regret it.

Counting Sheep in Craven:

1. Arn
2. Tarn
3. Tethera
4. Fethera
5. Pub
6. Aayther
7. Layather
8. Quoather
9. Quaather
10. Dugs
11. Arnadugs
12. Tarnadugs
13. Teheradugs
14. Fetheradugs
15. Buon
16. Arnabuon
17. Tarnabuon
18. Thetherabuon
19. Fetherabuon
20. Gun-a-gun

The Giant of Dalton Mill

At Dalton, in the parish of Topcliffe, there was formerly an old cornmill, with the miller's house attached. In front of the miller's house there was a long ridge, or mound, known as the 'Giant's Grave,' and in the mill was preserved a long, straight instrument, like a large sword, or straightened scythe-blade, believed to have been the giant's knife.

While the mill stood, these mementoes were visible for all to see the truth of the story of the Giant of Dalton Mill.

This giant had the same taste for bread made

of human bones as had the one, in a more familiar story, who is accused of declaring:

> *'Fee, Fi, Fo, Fum,*
> *I smell the blood of an Englishman*
> *Be he alive or be he dead,*
> *I'll grind his bones to make my bread'*

One day the giant of Dalton captured a youth, on the adjoining wilds of Pilmoor, whom he led home, and kept secluded in the mill, working as the giant's servant, but always denied freedom or time off.

Jack, the lad mentioned, was determined to have a holiday at the approaching Topcliffe fair. The fair day came, on one of the hot days of July, and, after a hearty meal, the giant lay down in the mill for his afternoon nap, still holding the knife with which he had been cutting his loaf of bone flour bread.

As sleep overpowered him, his fingers relaxed their hold of the weapon. Jack gently drew the knife from his grasp, and then, firmly raising it with both hands, drove the blade into the single eye of the monster. He awoke with a fearful howl, but had enough presence of mind to close the mill door, and so prevent the escape of his assailant. Jack was fairly trapped, but his native ingenuity came to his aid.

Being blinded, the giant could only grope for him. Jack, looking desperately for escape before the giant grabbed him, slayed the giant's dog, which was just rousing itself from sleep as the giant shouted. It took him but a few minutes to do this, and hurriedly take off its skin. This skin he then threw around himself, and, running on all fours and barking like the dog, he passed between the giant's legs, got to the door, and, unbarring it quickly, escaped.

The giant, mortally wounded, didn't last long after Jack's escape. Death claimed him shortly, but the grave and the knife survived in the mill to prove the story for years to come.

A folklore limerick from "Yorkshire Folk-lore", p. 142

There was an old woman at Baildon,

Whose door had a horseshoe nail'd on,

Because one night,

They'd had such a fright,

With a boggart that was a horned and tail'd 'un.

The Giant of Sessay

Up until the time of Henry VII, Sessay and the lands around were owned by the Darell family. At this point, the Darell's were left without a male heir, and the eldest daughter of the family, Joan Darell, took over the lands.

About the same time a strange monster began to haunt the woods around the village. He was a huge brute in human form, with legs like elephants' legs, arms of a similar size, and a face that was most fierce to look upon. He had only one eye, placed in the midst of his forehead, his mouth was as large as a lion's, and garnished with teeth as long as the prongs of a hayfork.

The only clothing he wore was a cow's hide fastened across his chest, while over his shoulder he usually carried as a weapon, a club formed of a stout young tree, torn up by the roots.

Now and then he made the woods ring with demoniacal laughter, now and then with the most savage, unearthly growls you have ever heard.

Like most giants of olden times he had a ravenous appetite, and daily he visited the tanners' herds and walked off with a choice heifer or fat ox under his arm, devouring it raw in his lair, a cave in the woods.

If he wanted a change of diet, he paid a visit to the neighbouring miller and stole a sack of oatmeal, drawn with his long arm through the mill window. This he took to his cave, and, mixing it in a large trough with the blood of the animals he had stolen, he ate the porridge thus made with a wonderful relish. But, worst of all, if he wanted a very choice morsel, he would carry off a delicate young maiden from some village home, or a child from its cradle.

This was no pleasant neighbour to have, and the inhabitants of Sessay, more than once, banded themselves together to destroy him, but all their efforts came to nothing.

Either they could not succeed in tracking

him to his den, or, if they did, the way in which he showed his enormous teeth, roared out his unearthly growls, or played with the young tree he carried in his hand, had such an effect that his would-be assailants made themselves scarce quicker than they came.

About this time there came a brave young soldier, who had taken an active part, and done wonderful things, in the wars abroad. Guy, son of Sir John D'Aunay paid a visit to Joan Darell, who was the daughter of an old friend of his father.

He found her occupied in the running her large and complicated estate and household. One of her difficulties was persuading any of her woodmen to go to the Woods for the necessary timber for fuel and building repairs. She was trying to persuade one so to do when D'Aunay arrived.

'I have heard,' said he, *'of this monster who so terrifies your servants, and devours your tenants' cattle, and even their children. Is it indeed true?'*

'Alas', she replied, *'it is only too true. But come in and take refreshments.'*

Now, young D'Aunay had come on an errand at which many young men evince a good deal of nervousness, and beating about the bush. But he went directly to the point, and told the strongminded spinster, the heiress of all the broad acres of the Darells, that he thought a union of the property of the Darells and D'Aunays would serve to build up a great family estate. Would she wed him, and make this happen?

She admired his honesty, and agreed on one condition, to prove that he deserved to marry the last of the Darells.

'Name the condition,' said he. *'I will undertake the task, whatever it may be.'*

She replied, *'Slay the monster who is desolating our fields and spreading such lamentation and woe over the village. Rid us of this brute, and my hand is yours.'*

'Willingly will I try', was the response, *'and if I fail, I shall fail in a good cause.'*

'See, there comes the giant', cried the lady, looking through the window and seeing the monster stalking out of the wood, with his tree trunk club over his shoulder, towards the mill.

'Truly he is a fearful adversary', exclaimed the champion, as he joined her at the window and proceeded to buckle on his sword.

On went the giant towards the mill, evidently set on fetching his usual sack of meal. The miller saw him and trembled, but took no steps to protect his property. The mill was one of those the top of which, with sails, turns on a pivot with the wind.

Suddenly, as the giant was drawing the sack out of the window, the wind changed, and swept the sails round to the side on which he was. Round came the arms, or sails, and one of them, catching the monster on the head, sent him stunned on his back to the ground. Young Sir Guy saw his opportunity, ran up, and, before the giant recovered his senses, drove his sword through the brute's one eye into his brain.

There were great rejoicings in the area all around Sessay. Next day an immense trench was dug, and the enormous carcase of the giant rolled into it and buried, amid shouts of thanks for Sir Guy.

Not many weeks afterwards the bells of Sessay rang merrily at the wedding of Joan Darell and young Sir Guy D'Aunays, from whom, I suppose, is descended family of that name, which still, I believe, owns the place.

The Golden Ball

From Yorkshire Folklore, VOL I (1888), pages 94-96. This was in a Yorkshire dialect, so have tinkered with the language but not the structure. Though I really like one of the original early lines "He'd gold on his cap, an' gold on his finger, gold on his neck, an' a red gold watch-chain - eh! but he had some brass"...

There was once two sisters, who after walking home through the fair, saw a handsome young man stood between them and their house. They'd never seen such a bonny lad before, and he was dripping in gold. He'd gold on his cap, wore golden rings on each finger, gold around his neck, and a thick gold watch-chain disappearing into his waistcoat pocket. Held out towards the lasses, in each hand, there was a golden ball. He gave one to each of them, but warned them that if they ever lost their ball, then they'd be hanged.

The youngest of the sisters, while playing catch by herself near a park wall, lost her ball over the wall. She ran to follow it, but as she rounded the wall, saw it roll across the last of grass and into the house. She couldn't get in to follow it, and no-one answered the door before men came to drag her away to answer for losing the ball. Her sweetheart promised he'd recover the ball before she could be hanged, and went to search for it himself. He found the gate locked, so started to climb over the wall. When he was right on top, an old woman came and stood in front of him and told him there was only one way to get the ball - he must spend three days in the house.

The lad agreed, and found the door to the house unlocked when he got there. He searched the house from top to bottom, but there was no sign of the golden ball anywhere. As night closed in, he heard movement outside in the courtyard.

Looking out through the window, the yard was as full of spirits as rotten meat is full of maggots. He heard steps coming upstairs next, so hid behind the door, keeping as still as a mouse.

A giant came into the room where he was hiding, five times as tall as the lad, he was, but luckily the giant didn't see him. Instead, he leant down to the window and looked out to the spirits outside in the yard, and as he leant on his elbows, the lad jumped out on him from behind and chopped him in half with his sword. The top of the giant fell down to the yard, and the bottom half stayed at the window, as though still looking outside.

There was a great cry from the spirits outside when they saw half their master come tumbling down, and they called out "*There comes half our master, give us t'other half.*"

So the lad said, "*It's no use o'thee, a pair of legs standing alone, so go join your brother*", and he threw the bottom half of the giant out of the window.

As soon as the legs hit the yard, the spirits went quiet.

The next night, the lad stopped at the house again, and a second giant came in at the door. The lad was expecting this, and as it entered, he swung his sword, chopping the second giant in half. This took the giant so much by surprise that the legs carried on walking across the room and up the chimney. "*Get thee after the legs*", said the lad, and threw the head up the chimney too.

The third night, no giant appeared, so the lad got into one of the beds. As he started to drop to sleep, he heard the spirits moving underneath the bed, rolling the ball back and forth between them. He quietly lifted his sword and knelt up, and when one of the spirits moved his leg out from under the bed, he quickly chopped it off. Another spirit stuck its arm out from the other side of the bed, and he cut that off too. As the spirits squirmed under the bed, trying to keep away from the sword, they pushed each other into his reach, so the lad maimed them one by one, until they plucked up enough courage to flee together, wailing and wailing as one. This left him free to pick up the golden ball they had left under the bed, and go off to seek his true love.

The lass had been taken to York to be hanged, and as she was brought out to the scaffold she cried out:

> *"Stop, stop; I think I see my mother coming.*
> *Oh mother, have you got my golden ball,*
> *And are you coming to set me free?"*
>
> *"I've neither got thy golden ball,*
> *Nor come to set you free,*
> *But I have come to see thee hung,*
> *Upon this gallow tree."*

The hangman told her to say her prayers and be ready to be hanged by the neck until she was dead. But in return she said:

"Stop, stop: I think I see my father coming.
Oh father, have you got my golden ball,
And are you coming to set me free?"

"I've neither got thy golden ball,
Nor come to set you free,
But I have come to see thee hung,
Upon this gallow tree."

So the hangman told her to hurry with her prayers so he could get on with it, and to get her neck in the noose. But again, she said to stop, excusing herself as she saw her brother, her sister, her uncle and aunt, even her cousin coming to save her. The hangman had had enough, thinking she was just playing games to delay the inevitable and told her that her time was up. Just then, she spotted her sweetheart coming through the crowd, holding the golden ball above his head, she cried out one last time:

"Stop, stop: I see my sweetheart coming.
Sweetheart, have you brought my golden ball,
And come to set me free?"

"Aye, I've brought thy golden ball,
And come to set you free,
I have not come to see thee hung,
Upon the gallow tree."

Needless to say, she was allowed down from the scaffold and took better care of the golden ball from then on.

A curse:

You go out at night, every night, until you find nine toads. When you've gotten nine toads, you tie them up with string, make a hole and bury the toads in that hole. As the toads pine away, so the person you have looked upon with an evil eye pines away, until they die without any disease at all!

The Golden Cradle and Castle Hill

One cold morning, right at the start of February, not so long ago, George woke up early. It was still dark and George didn't need to be anywhere that morning, but he couldn't get back to sleep. So up he got, checked on his sheep, and took Stanley the dog out for a walk.

Up Castle Hill he went, on that cold, foggy morning. On top of the hill, it was as if they were on an island, with the rest of the area hidden by the fog.

Stanley suddenly stopped chasing imaginary rabbits and stood still, barking at something George couldn't see. As George got closer to him, he saw a stone staircase spiralling down into the hill, a staircase he was sure he hadn't seen before. Intrigued, he told Stanley to stay put while he took a look.

Down the staircase he went, dark for a moment, and then lighter as a faint glow came from moss covering the staircase walls.

The stairs ended in a wide cavern, and George's attention was drawn to a golden object in the centre of the space. He walked towards it and found a small cradle, like a newborn baby would sleep in, made of gold. He reached out to touch it, but before he could, a voice sounded out. A rich, powerful, old voice.

'I'm Brigid, and that is my golden cradle. The Brigantes gave it to me when they built the fort on this hill, so I would protect the high ground. Within it they placed their most valued daughter to stay with me within the hill. In return, for hundreds of years I protected them. Even when the Romans came, they didn't touch the fort, it was safe under my care. Then the new gods came and my people drifted away and stopped worshipping me. Still, I protected them. Until the people thought the new priests might like the gold for their *god. They came back to me, within the hill, and tried to steal away my golden cradle, my price for protection. So I sent their daughter back to them, with*

fire and destruction as their reward. She left their lands scorched and barren, their livestock and stores destroyed, and the stones of their fort melting like wax. Few have dared to return to me since then, with the path only open on my day each year, when they used to feast in my honour. Have you come for the cradle? Perhaps you should meet the Brigante's daughter?'

The voice faded and a slithering noise came from the steps George had just walked down. He turned to see two red eyes burning in the low light, smoke curling from wide nostrils, and the first coils of a huge serpent coming around the spiral steps.

George panicked. He didn't know what to do, or where to go. The way he came in was completely blocked. But while he stood frozen in place for those first moments, he heard barking from the side of the cavern. He dashed towards the noise and found a narrow tunnel which he dived into. He wriggled, he crawled, he squirmed.

As fast as he could, he made his way towards the barking, fearful that any moment he'd feel the hot breath of the serpent on his feet.

After what seemed like an eternity, but must have been only a few minutes, his head popped out into fresh air and he dropped a few feet onto the hill side. Stanley was there, barking to guide him back to safety.

They rushed back from the hill as fast as they could, and though they've been back many times since, George has never found the stone stairs again. That said, he's made sure never to go back before dawn, and never on the 1st February…

A Grassington Bargest

This account comes from "Billy" in around 1881, as reported in the Leeds Mercury Supplement, February 28th, 1881. The dialect has been softened a little below, but beyond that it has been kept the same.

"You see, sir," said Billy, "as how I'd been a-clock- dressing at Gerston (Grassington), an' I'd stayed rather late, an' maybe getting a little sup o' spirit, but I was far from bein' drunk, an' knaw'd everything 't pass'd. It were about eleven o'clock when I left, an' were at back end o' t' year ; an' it were a grand neet.

T' moon were very bright, an' I never saw Rylston Fell plainer i' a' my life. Now, you see, sir, I were passin' down t' mill lane, an' I heard summut come past me, brush, brush, brush, wi' chains rattlin' a' t' while; but I saw nowt ; an' thought to mysen', now, this is a most mortal queer thing.

An' I then stood still, an' looked about me, but I saw nowt at a', nobbut t' two stone walls on each side o' t' mill lane.

Then I heard again this brush, brush, brush wi' t' chains; for, you see, when I stood still it stopp'd; an' then, thought I, this must be a Bargest, that so much is said about.

I hurried on toward t' wood brig, for they say as how this Bargest cannot cross water; but, lord, sir, when I got over t' brig, I heard this same thing again ; so it would either have cross'd t' water, or gone round by t' spring head (thirty miles!). An' then I became a valiant man, for I were a bit frightened afore; an', thinks I, I'll turn an' have a peep at this thing.

So I went up Greet Bank towards Linton, an' heard this brush, brush, brush wi' t' chains a' t' way, but I saw nowt; then it stopp'd a' of a sudden. So I turned back to go home, but I'd hardly reached t' door when I heard again this brush, brush, brush, an' t' chains, going down towards t' Holin House, an' I followed it, an' t' moon then shone really bright, an' I saw its tail. Then, thought I, thou old thing! I can say I've seen the' now, so I'll away home.

When I got to t' door there was a great thing like a sheep, but it were bigger, liggin' across t' threshold o' t' door, an' it were woolly like; an', says I, "*Get up,*" an' it wouldn't get up; then, says I, "*Stir thyself*" an' it wouldn't stir itself. An' I grew valiant, an' raised t' stick to baste it up, an' then it looked at me, an' such eyes they did glower at me. They were as big as saucers, an' like a cruel ball; first there were a red ring, then a blue one, then a white one; an' these rings grew less an' less, 'till they came to a dot.

Now, I wasn't scared of it, tho' it grinned at me fearfully; an' I kept on saying, "*Get up an' stir thyself*"; an' t' wife heard as how I were at t' door, an' she came to open it, an' then this thing got up an' walked off, for it were more feared o' t' wife than it were of me!

An' I called t' wife, an' she said it were t' Bargest, but ah've never seen it since; an' that's a true story."

The Hand of Glory

Stanmore is a wild moorland district west of Bowes, and extending to the borders of Westmoreland. Across the wild waste runs the road from Bowes to Brough, and connecting North Yorkshire with Westmoreland. On a ridge, near the centre of this moorland tract, a fragment of Rere Cross, or Rey Cross (an old boundary cross), yet stands, and near to it is Spital House, no doubt the site of an old hospital for wayfarers, and, in more modern times, an inn.

In 1797 A.D., this inn is said to have been kept by one George Alderson, who, with his wife, and their maid-of-all-work, Bella, managed the establishment.

The inn at that time consisted of a long, narrow building, standing with one end to the highroad. The lower story was used as stabling for the horses of the stage-coaches, which crossed this wild moor on their way from York to Carlisle.

The upper story was reached by a flight of steps leading up from the road to a stout oaken door. The deeply-recessed windows were all barred with stout iron bars.

One cold October night, the red curtains were drawn across the windows, and a huge log-fire sputtered and crackled on the broad hearth, and lighted up the faces of George Alderson and his son, as they sat talking of their gains at the fair of Brough Hill; these gains, representing a large sum of money, being safely stowed away in a cupboard in the landlord's bedroom.

Mrs. Alderson and Bella sat a little way off spinning by fire-light, for the last coach had gone by, and the house door was barred and bolted for the night.

Outside, the wind and rain were having a battle: there came fierce gusts which made the old casements rattle, and stirred the red curtains, and then a torrent of rain swept smartly across the window, striking the glass so angrily that it seemed as if the small panes must shatter under its violence.

Into the midst of this fitful disturbance, only varied by the men's voices beside the hearth, there came a knock at the door.

"*Open t' door, lass*," said Alderson. "*I wouldn't keep a dog outside on a night like this.*"

"'*Eh! Best slacken the chain, lass,*" said the more cautious landlady.

The girl went to the door; but when she saw that the visitor was an old woman, she opened the door wide and bade her come in. There entered a bent figure, dressed in a long cloak and hood; this last was drawn over her face, and as she walked feebly to the armchair which Alderson pushed forward, the rain streamed from her clothing and made a pool on the oaken floor. She shivered violently, and refused to take off her cloak and have it dried. She also refused the offer of food or a bed. She said she was on her way to the north, and must start as soon as there was daylight. All she wanted was a rest beside the fire: she could get the sleep she needed in her armchair.

The innkeeper and his wife were well used to wayfarers, and they soon said "*Good-night*," and went to bed; so did their son. Bella was left alone with the shivering old woman. The girl had kept silence, but now she put her wheel away in its corner, and began to talk. She only got surly answers, and, although the voice was low and subdued, the girl fancied that it did not sound like a woman's. Presently the wayfarer stretched out her feet to warm them, and Bella's quick eyes saw under the hem of the skirts that the stranger wore horseman's gaiters. The girl felt uneasy, and instead of going to bed, she resolved to stay up and watch.

"*I'm sleepy*," she said, yawning; but the figure in the chair made no answer. Presently Bella lay down on a long settle, beyond the range of firelight, and watched the stranger, while she pretended to fall asleep.

All at once the figure in the chair stirred, raised its head, and listened; then it rose slowly to its feet, no longer bent, but tall and powerful-looking. It stood listening for some time. There was no sound but Bella's heavy breathing, and the wind and the rain beating on the windows.

The woman took from the folds of her cloak a brown, withered, human hand; next she produced a candle, lit it from the fire, and placed it in the hand. Bella's heart beat so fast that she could hardly keep up the regular deep breathing of pretended sleep; but now she saw the stranger coming towards her with this ghastly chandelier, and she closed her lids tightly. She felt that the woman was bending over her, and that the light was passed slowly before her eyes, while these words were muttered in the strange masculine voice that had first roused her suspicions:

"Let those who rest more deeply sleep;
Let those awake their vigils keep."

The light moved away, and through her eyelashes Bella saw that the woman's back was turned to her, and that she was placing the hand in the middle of the long oak table, while she muttered this rhyme:

"Oh, Hand of Glory shed thy light,
Direct us to our spoil tonight."

Then she moved a few steps away, and undrew the window curtain. Coming back to the table, she said:

"Flash out thy blaze, O skeleton hand,
And guide the feet of our trusty band."

At once the light shot up a bright livid gleam, and the woman walked to the door; she took down the bar, drew back the bolts, unfastened the chain, and Bella felt a keen blast of cold night air rush in as the door was flung open. She kept her eyes closed, however, for the woman at that moment looked back at her, and drawing something from her gown, she blew a long, shrill whistle; she then went out at the door, and down a few of the steps, stopped, and whistled again; but the next moment a vigorous push sent her spinning down the steps into the road below, the door was closed, barred and bolted, and Bella almost flew to her master's bedroom, and tried to wake him in vain. He and his wife slept on, while their snores sounded loudly through the house.

The girl felt frantic! Then she tried to rouse young Alderson, but he slept as if in a trance. Now a fierce battery on the door, and cries below the windows, told that the band had arrived. A new thought came to Bella. She ran back to the kitchen. There was the Hand of Glory, still burning with a wonderful light. The girl caught up a cup of milk that stood on the table, dashed it on the flame, and extinguished it. In one moment, as it seemed to her, she heard footsteps coming from the bedrooms, and George Alderson and his son rushed into the room with firearms in their hands.

As soon as the robbers heard his voice bidding them depart, they summoned the landlord to open his doors, and produce his valuables. Meanwhile, young Alderson had opened the window, and for answer he fired his blunderbuss down among the men below.

There was a groan, a fall, then a pause, and, as it seemed to the besieged, some sort of discussion. Then a voice called out: "*Give up the Hand of Glory, and we will not harm you.*" For answer, young Alderson fired again, and the party drew off.

Seemingly they had trusted entirely to the Hand of Glory to keep them safe and unobserved.

The Hare and the Witch

Two similar stories of witches follow here, so it seemed sensible to put them together!

In the neighbourhood of Eskdale there was a young plantation, among the young trees of which great havoc was committed by the hares. Many of these were shot; but there was one old hare which neither shot could hurt nor snare could hold, and night after night it defiantly returned to its depredations.

At length a wise-man was consulted, and by his advice a silver coin was cut up into small pieces, and with this silver shot a gun was loaded. This did its work, and the hare was killed. But at the same time, an old woman suspected of witchcraft, and who lived at some distance, was engaged in her occupation of carding wool. Suddenly she threw up her hands, and shrieking out, "*They have shot my familiar spirit!*", she fell down dead.

In another dale, higher up the Esk, there was a hare which baffled all the grey-hounds that were slipped at her. They seemed to have no more chance with her than if they coursed the wind.

There was at the time a noted witch residing near, and her advice was asked about this wonderful hare. She seemed to have little to say about it, however, only she thought they had better let it be; but, above all, they must take care not to let a black dog loose at it.

Nevertheless, either from recklessness or from defiance, the party did go out coursing soon after with a black dog. The dog was slipped, and they perceived at once that the hare was at a disadvantage. She made as soon as possible for a stone wall, and endeavoured to escape through a sheep-hole at the bottom. Just as she reached this hole the dog threw himself upon her and caught her in the haunch, but was unable to hold her. She got through, and was seen no more.

The sportsmen, either in bravado or from terror of the consequences, went straight to the house of the witch to inform her of what had happened. They found her in bed hurt, she said, by a fall; but the wound looked very much as if it had been produced by the teeth of a dog, and it was on a part of the woman corresponding to that by which the hare had been seized by the black hound before their eyes.

Whether this wise-woman recovered from the effect of the accident, I do not know; but a Guisborough witch, who died within the memory of man, was lame for several years, in consequence, it was said, of a bite she received from a dog, while slipping through the key-hole of her own door in the shape of a hare.

Janet's Cove

Well, I reckon I've told this story before, Grannie began, but when I was a lass I lived up Malham way. My father had a farm close by Gordale Scar, and it's a strange country around there. Great rocks on all sides where only goats can climb, becks flowing underground and then bubbling up in the fields.

On the other side of our steading, was a cove that folks called Janet's Cove. They told all sorts of tales about it and reckoned it was plagued by boggarts. But they couldn't keep me away from it, it was the prettiest spot in the dale, and I never got bored wandering around by the water and among the rowans. There was a waterfall in the cove, with a dark cave behind it, and it was overhung with ash and hazel trees.

One night I was sitting up for my father until 4 o'clock in the morning. It was the day before Easter Sunday and my father was desperately busy with lambing. He hadn't taken his shoes and socks off for a week! He'd doze a little by the fire, and then wake up, light the lantern, and go out to check on the sheep. He let me wait up for him, so I could warm him a spot of tea over the fire. But when the clock struck 4, he said I must go to bed. He'd take a turn around the croft, then set off to the barn, to milk the cows.

But I didn't want to go to bed, I'd been dozing off and on all night, and I wasn't feeling a little bit tired. So when my father had set off, I went to the door and looked outside. My, it was a grand night! The moon had just turned full, and was lighting up the stones in the meadow, the becks were like sliver, and the old yew-trees that grow on the face of the scar had long shadows as black as pitch. I stood there on the threshold for maybe five minutes, and then said to myself, *"I'll just run down as far as Janet's Cove before I go to bed."*

It was only two or three minutes walk, and before long I was sat amongst the rocks, and the moon was glistening through the ash trees and onto the water. I must have dropped off to sleep for best part of an hour, because before I knew it the moon was setting, and I could see that dawn wasn't far off. I reckoned I'd better get back home to my bed, but just then I saw something moving on the far side of the beck. At first, I thought it was just a sheep, but when I looked closer I saw I was wrong, it was a lass about the same size as myself.

Strangest thing about the lass was that she was naked, as naked as a hen's egg, and that at five o'clock on a frosty April morning! It made me shiver to see her standing there with not even a shawl to warm her back.

Well, I crept close to a large stone and kept my eye on her. First of all, she moved down to the water and stood in it, then started splashing water all over herself, like a bird washing itself in the beck. Then she climbed to the waterfall and let the water flow all over her face and shoulders. I could see her body shining through the water and her yellow hair streaming out on both sides of her head. After a while she climbed onto a rock in the middle of the beck and grabbed hold of the branch of an ash. She broke off a stick, shaped it into a sort of wand, and started waving it in the air.

Now, up to that point, everything in the cove was a silent as the grave. I could hear the cockerels crowing up at our house, but all the wild birds were still roosting and fast asleep. But no sooner did this lass start waving her wand, than the larks started singing. The fields had been full of sleeping larks, and they'd all taken flight above our heads at the same time, singing their hearts out. She then pointed her wand at the moors, and the curlews started singing. When she heard them, she started laughing, and splashing the water with her foot.

All the while, she kept beating time to the bird song with her wand. Sometimes she pointed it to the curlews on the moor, sometimes to fields, and then, suddenly, to the hazels and rowan bushes by the beck-side. Before I knew what was happening, the blackbirds woke up and started whistling like mad. It sounded like there must be a blackbird for every bush along the beck. The birds kept at it for several minutes, then the lass made a fresh movement with her wand, and the robins began to try and drown out the songs of the blackbirds.

She always seemed to know whose turn was next, and where every type of bird was roosting. One minute she pointed her wand to the top of the trees and I heard "*caw, caw*", the next she pointed towards the mossy roots of the trees near the beck and a Jenny wren hopped out and sang as though it was fit to burst.

All the while, it was getting lighter, and lighter, and I could see that the sun was shining on the cliffs above Malham, even though the cove was still in shade. I knew my mother would soon by looking for me in bed, and I started wondering what she'd say when she found it empty. I was a tad afraid when I thought that, but I couldn't take my eyes off the lass with the wand. I was fair bewitched by her, and I reckon that if she pointed at me, I would have started singing!

However, she never clapped eyes on me sat behind the stone, she was far too busy with the birds, and getting more excited every minute. By now the birdsong was deafening, I'd never heard anything like it before or since.

The sun cleared the top of the fell, and shone down into the cove. Janet saw it, and when it was shining like a great golden ball at the top of the hill, she pointed her wand at it. I looked at her, and looked at the sun too, and was amazed to see the sun was dancing too! I rubbed my eyes to see if I'd made a mistake, but sure enough, there was the little naked lass making the sun dance like mad with her. Then, all of a sudden, I remembered that it was Easter Sunday, and I'd heard tell that the sun always dances on Easter morning.

When she'd danced with the sun a while, she seemed to forget about the birds. She let her wand drop and climbed down the waterfall. Then she sat herself on a rock behind the fall, and clapped her hands together and laughed. I looked at her and I saw the prettiest sight I'd ever set eyes on.

By now the sun was high in the sky, and was shining straight up the beck onto the waterfall. Water was spraying up as it fell onto the rocks, and a rainbow formed across the fall. There, plain as life, was Janet sat on a rock right in the middle of the rainbow, with all the colours shining on her hair.

I fair lost track of time, sat there, wrapped in my shawl, staring at Janet, at the sun, at the waterfall, until I heard someone calling me. It was my father, and then I knew that folks had missed me up at the farm and were looking for me. When I realised that, I shot off like a rabbit, straight to my father who was stood between the cove and our house, shouting for me as loud as he could.

A Kilnsay Fairy Dance

The late Daniel Cooper was a great spotter of fairies. He used to relate that one moonlight night, as he was returning from Kilnsay, he took a footpath across the fields. He there saw a lot of fairies dancing in a field that was rented by himself. On the following morning his avocation of a market gardener led him to the site of the dance, when he found the ground covered with mushrooms of the genuine sort. Daniel said there was a slight breeze on the preceding evening, and a few thorn bushes grew near the spot. "*What!*" said he, "*after all, my fairies might be only mushrooms which seemed to stir from the moonlight shadows of the waving branches falling over them!*"

At this time Daniel had an old maiden aunt who resided in his house. She was well informed, but was exceedingly superstitious, and an expert in fairy folk-lore. She would not accept Daniel's interpretation. "*My dear*," she said, "*you saw the fairies, and the mushrooms were a gift to you, because you were good, and did not disturb the dance."*

It was a common belief in Craven that mushrooms are made by the fairies.

The Legend of Semerwater

A long time ago, in the spot where the great lake Semerwater, source of the river Bain, now occupies, was once a fair sized town.

One day an old man came to the town. He was scruffy, his clothes not much more than rags, and dirty from many months spent on the road.

He knocked on the first door he came to and ask for food, but they turned him away. He moved through the town, knocking on every door to ask for a meal and a drink. Each household told him the same. He was not welcome, and they would give him nothing.

As he got to the far end of town, he tried the very last house. It was a small and humble cottage, with an aged and poverty stricken couple. He repeated his request to these, and unlike the others, they invited him in.

They didn't have much to share, but offered him all they could. A small bowl of stew, some bread, and some freshly drawn water to drink.

What's more, they invited him to stay the night, dry and safe in their cottage, before continuing on his journey the next day.

When he left in the morning, he stood by the door of the cottage where he'd been welcomed in, and, looking back over the hard-hearted, uncharitable town, lifted up his hands and repeated the following lines:

'Semerwater rise! Semerwater sink !

And swallow the town, all save this house, where they gave me meat and drink'

No sooner said than done. The waters of the valley rose, the town sunk and the houses disappeared beneath them.

But as they approached the hospitable cottage, the waves stopped short. Even now, you can see a small old house near the lower end of the lake, which is all that is left of the once flourishing town.

On some days, if you look carefully through

the waters, you may yet see the roofs and chimneys of the other houses at the bottom of the lake.

Hob rhyme (2):

Hob trush Hob! Where is thou?
Ah's tying on mah left fuit shoe
An' Ah'll be wi' thee noo.

Hob rhyme (3):

Gin Hob mun hae nowght
Bud a hardin hamp,
He'll cum nae mair,
Nowther to berry nor stamp

Linfit Leadboilers

There are three stories told about local villagers around Huddersfield. One crops up in a few other places around the country (The Marsden Cuckoo), one seems to be so common across the country that it isn't worth repeating here (Slaithwaite / Slawitt moon-rakers), and the Linfit Leadboilers. I've not come across the "leadboilers" anywhere else, so it could be a genuinely local one!

A few hundred years ago, the moors around the Colne Valley were used for musket practice by soldiers stationed nearby.

Villagers recognised their chance to make a little money on the side and collected the lead bullets from around the targets on the moor. Unfortunately, they weren't too bright and tried to melt the lead in a large cauldron of water before selling it on.

Ever since then, the people of Linthwaite (Linfit) have been known as "Leadboilers".

Quoted in Briggs, but originally from Cornhill Magazine, Vol IX (1864) in an article called "Yorkshire", so I'm taking this as being from Yorkshire!

One day two lads were busy robbing an orchard; one was aloft in a damson plum-tree, pulling the fruit at random; the other at the foot was engaged in hot haste; stuffing them into his pockets, and from time to time hurriedly bolting one down his throat. Silence and expedition being imperatively incumbent in the situation, the first had not much time to select which to gather, nor the other what to put in his mouth. Suddenly the lad inquired fearfully of the one above, *"Tom! Has plummocks legs?"*, *"Noa"*, roared Tom. *"Then"*, said Bill, with a manly despair, *"then I ha' swallowed a straddly-beck."* (Frog.)

The Marsden Cuckoo

In times gone by, when time was tracked by the ebb and flow of the seasons, rather than strict calendar dates, the folk of Marsden used to look forward to hearing the first cuckoo of Spring. They knew that once the cuckoo had arrived, the grass and heather would start to grow once more, and their sheep and cattle would have plenty to eat. There would be gentler weather to work in, the days would be warmer, lighter and longer, and it would be altogether more pleasant than the colder winter months.

One year, a group of villagers decided that they would cheat the seasons. Instead of letting the cuckoo depart, they would trap it in Marsden and ensure the gentler weather stayed forever.

They collected stone together for wall building, and waited for a cuckoo to arrive in a small field, bounded by a dry stone wall. As soon as they saw the cuckoo, the villagers worked hard, raising the wall around the field.

The cuckoo watched for a short while, singing away as the villagers worked on the wall. After a while, it took off, circling the field, then flew away low, just skimming over the top of the wall. This proved to the locals that it was 'nobbut a course too low', and they had nearly trapped the cuckoo and ensured that Spring would last forever…

To this day, they celebrate the first cuckoo of Spring in Marsden each April.

Melch Dick

What I'm going to tell you now is what I've heard my mother say, scores of times, so you'll know it's true. It was the back end of the year, and the lads had gone into the woods to gather hazelnuts and acorns. There were two or three big lads amongst them, but most were little 'uns, and one was lame in the leg. They called him Doed of Billy's of Claypit Lane.

Well, the lads had gotten a load of the nuts, and the they set off home as fast as they could go, as it were getting a bit dusky in the wood. But little Doed couldn't keep up with the other lads on account of his dodgy leg. So the lads kept hollering back to him to look sharp and get a shift on, or he'd get left behind.

So Doed loped along as fast as he was able, but he couldn't keep up with the other lads, try as he might, and all the time the light was slowly fading. At long length he thought he saw one of the lads waiting for him under an oak tree, but when he drew closer he realised it was someone that he'd never clapped eyes on before. He was no bigger than Doed, but it was hard to tell how old he was, and he had a weird smell about him – as though he'd taken the essence of all the trees from the wood and smeared them over his body. But what capped it all off were the clothes he was dressed in, covered in green moss, and on his head was a cap of red fur.

Well, when Doed saw him he was a bit afraid, but the lad looked a him in a friendly way and said, *"Now then Doed, where are you going?"*

"I'm off home", says Doed, and his teeth started to chatter with fright.

"Well, I'm going your way", says the lad, *"so if you like you can come along with me. You'll not recognise me, but I can tell who you are by the way you favour your mother. You'll have heard tell of your uncle, Ned Bowker, that lives over by Sally Abbey? He's my father, so I reckon we're cousins."*

Now, Doed had heard his mother tell him about his Uncle Ned, so he calmed down a little, but still wasn't keen on the look of this lad. However, they carried on talking and Doed let on that he was keen on squirrels. You see, he loved to collect animals and kept linnets, and magpies, in cages, and a box full of hedgehogs. But he'd never caught a squirrel, they were too quick for him, and he wanted one more than anything in the world.

When Melch Dick heard that – for of course the lad was Melch Dick himself – he said that if Doed came with him, he'd soon give him what he wanted. He'd been climbing trees and caught a squirrel, putting it in the basket he'd carried his dinner in.

Well, little Doed hardly knew what to do. It was getting late, and there was something about this lad that worried him. But then he thought of the squirrel and how much he wanted him. So he said to Melch Dick that he'd go with to fetch the squirrel, but he mustn't stop long or folks would know that he'd lost his way and would come looking for him.

When Melch Dick heard him say he'd come with him, his eyes glistened, and he set off through the wood with Doed following him. The wood was full of great oak trees, with birch set amongst them that there just beginning to change colour.

After a while they got to a pool in the middle of the wood. It was no bigger than a duck pond, but the water was deep, and all around the pond was a ring of Aspen trees with their boughs hanging over the water. The sky had been overcast earlier, but the wind had cleared the clouds, and the moon was shining in a way that lit up the trees and made the water glisten like silver.

Melch Dick settled down by the water and Doed did the same, as they started talking again, with Doed asking him why he was covered in green moss.

"If you were to climb trees the same as I have", answered Melch Dick, *"then you'd be covered with moss too, I'd say."*

"And why do you wear a cap of red fur?"

"Why shouldn't I wear a fur cap, I'd like to know? My mother makes them from squirrel skins, and they're fearful warm in winter time."

When little Doed heard mention of squirrels again, it reminded him to ask for the squirrel in the basket.

"Wait a while", said Melch Dick, *"and I'll show you more squirrels than you've ever seen in all your life."*

With that, he takes a penny whistle out of his pocket, obviously made by Melch Dick himself, whittled from a slim ash branch. He put it to his mouth, and blew two or three notes, and sure enough, there was some noise from nearby and in no time at all, half a dozen squirrels were sat on the branches of the aspens. When Doed saw the squirrels in the moonlight, he was beside himself with excitement. He looked at them, they looked at him, and their eyes were as bright as glow-worms.

All the while Melch Dick playing his whistle, and the squirrels kept coming through the trees. You could hardly see the branches for the squirrels now. It was as though all the squirrels in the forest had heard the tune and been forced to follow the sound. They mad no noise or fuss, but sat down on the branches, pricked up their ears, cocked their tails over their backs, and kept their eyes fixed on Melch Dick.

Well, when Melch Dick decided he'd gathered enough squirrels, he changed his tune, and it was a rough tune too. Sometimes it was like the howling of the wind down a chimney, sometimes like the curlews and lapwings up on the moors. But when the squirrels heard the tune, they lined up twelve to a branch. They jumped from tree to tree, right around the pool, with their tails set straight out behind them. They were that close together, it was like a great coil of rope spinning around the water, all the time their faces turned to Melch Dick, and their eyes were blazing like burning coals. Round and round they went, with little Doed just holding his breath and watching them. He'd seen horses riding around a ring at a fair, but that was nothing compared to the squirrels spinning around the pool.

After a while, Doed thought that Melch Dick would stop playing, but he did nothing of the sort. Instead, he played ever faster keeping one eye on the squirrels and one on little Doed. The faster he played, the faster the squirrels jumped, and before long the tune was more like a shriek than a dance tune. Doed had heard nothing like it before, it was as though all the devils in hell and had loose and were being blown through the sky above. It was a strange sound, and a strange sight too, and little Doed's teeth started chattering and every limb on his body was shaking like the aspen leaves on the trees around the pool.

Doed was scared half to death, but for all that, he couldn't take his eyes off the squirrels, they'd bewitched him, had the squirrels. He put his hand to his head, and it felt as though he was spinning around and around himself. Now, that was what Melch Dick wanted, and why he'd set the squirrels going. He couldn't do anything to Doed while he was master of his own senses, but if he was to get giddy enough to drift off into a daydream, then sure enough, Melch Dick would have him in his power and be able to turn him into a squirrel, as he had done to so many lads and lasses before.

As Doed felt his head getting woolly, thinking he was falling asleep and unsure where he was any more, he decided he must be lying in bed at home, drifting off to sleep without saying his prayers. You see, his mother had taught him a prayer to say every night before going to bed. Well, Doed tried to say his prayer, but couldn't remember the words! That made him uneasy, as he was a good lad and it worried him that he forgotten the words. All that he could call to mind was something that he'd heard the lads and lasses say on their way home from school. He reckoned it was more a bit of fun than a prayer, but he started to say it anyway, as loud as he could:

"Mathew, Mark, Luke, and John,
Bless the bed that I lie on."

He'd no sooner said the words than all of a sudden, Melch Dick stopped playing, the squirrels stopped jumping, the bats stopped flying over the pool, the moon hid behind a great thunder cloud, and the wood and the water were as black as a boot. Then there came a scuffling and a shrieking all over the wood. The squirrels started spitting and swearing like mad, the wind yowled, and there were all sorts of strange noises overhead. Then, after a minute of chaos, the moon came clear of the cloud, and Doed looked around. But there was nothing to see. Melch Dick was no longer next to him, and there was not a squirrel left in the trees. All that he could see what the aspen leaves blowing in the wind, and tiny waves in the pond lapping against the bank.

Doed was well-nigh starved to death with cold and hunger, and the poor lad started crying as though his heart would break. But then he had enough sense to start shouting for help, and before long there came an answer. His father and the lads from the village had been looking for him all over the wood, and as soon as they found him, they took him home and put him to bed. It was a long while before he was better, and he never set foot in the wood again without a bit of witchwood in his pocket, cut from a rowan-tree on St Helen's day.

The Old Woman of Lexhoe

An old woman of Lexhoe appeared after her death to a farmer nearby, and informed him that, beneath a certain tree in his apple orchard, he would find a hoard of gold and silver which she had buried there.

He was to take a spade and dig it up, keep the silver for his trouble, but give the gold to a niece of hers who was then living in great poverty, and whose place of abode she pointed out.

At daybreak, after his dream or vision, the farmer went to the spot indicated, dug, and found the treasure, but kept it all to himself, though the sum allotted to him was considerable, and might have satisfied him.

From that day, however, he never knew rest or happiness. Though a sober man before, he took to drinking, but all in vain — his conscience gave him no rest.

Every night, at home or abroad, old Nanny's

ghost failed not to dog his steps, and reproach him with his faithlessness. At last, one Saturday evening, the neighbours heard him returning from Stokesley Market very late; his horse was galloping furiously, and as he left the high road to go into the lane which led to his own house, he never stopped to open the gate at the entrance of the lane, but cleared it with a bound. As he passed a neighbour's house, its inmates heard him screaming out "*I will, I will, I will*".

Looking out, they saw a little old woman in black, with a large straw hat on her head, whom they recognised as old Nanny, seated behind the terrified man on the runaway nag, and clinging to him closely. The farmer's hat was off, his hair stood on end, as he fled past them, uttering his fearful cry, "I *will, I will, I will*".

But when the horse reached the farm all was still, for the rider was a corpse.

Our Lady's Well

There's a well in North Yorkshire, at Threshfield, called Our Lady's Well, which has always been known as a safe haven from any supernatural creatures.

Late one night, a Threshfield man was on his way home after a few drinks when he stumbled across a group of fairy creatures dancing near his path. Knowing they would be angry if they spotted him watching, he froze – silent and still, but fascinated by their dance.

Suddenly, however, he let out an enormous sneeze.

Instantly the dance stopped and the creatures ran toward him. The local man sprinted towards Our Lady's Well, hoping he could make it there before they caught him.

He made it there by the skin of his teeth, leaping into the well to be sure of his safety. Once in, he was out of their reach, as they couldn't set foot with twenty yards of the well itself. However, they took their revenge by waiting in a circle around him until dawn, keeping him cold, wet and trapped until the sun shone its light upon them all.

The Potato and the Pig

Abe Ingham was a Horsforth allotment holder, and this is a story he told about his plot. He was digging up some potatoes one year, and was almost at the end of a row when his fork hit something large. At first he thought it was a great big stone he'd missed when digging over the plot in spring, but it was a potato bigger than his head!

He managed to get it out of the ground, and stood there catching his breath and staring at the giant potato. While he rested, a stranger came up to him. He was a young lad by the size of him, but he had an old look about his face.

The lad looked at the giant potato and asked Abe what he was going to do with it.

"I reckon I'll take it t'Flower Show an' get first prize", Abe replied.

"You mustn't do anything of the sort", said the lad, *"you must bury it. Get it back in the ground and see what it grows into."*

Well, Abe reckoned there might be something in that. If he could raise a sack of seed potatoes from it, he'd make a fortune! But it was the wrong time of year to be planting potatoes, of course.

"But where's the sense of setting a potato at t'back-end?"

"You'll not have to wait long to see what comes on it", he was told, and the lad walked off.

So Abe stuck in back in the ground and went home. That night it started raining and kept it up for days, so it was a week until he made it back to his allotment again. All that week he couldn't get the lad out of his head and his old looking green eyes kept staring back at him in his imagination.

He finally got back to his plot and right where the potatoes should have been there was a pig sty, with a great fat pig ready to slaughter. Amazed, he took a good look at the pig, then turned around to see the strange lad who'd told him to plant the potato.

"Well", he said, *"is there owt wrong with the pig?"*

"Nay, nowt wrong, but how did it get there?"

"He'll have come out of that potato you set in the ground last week." He looked at me with his green eyes and started grinning *"but you'd better plant the pig the same as you planted the potato."*

"Bury the pig!" I exclaimed. *"I'd sooner bury the missus. I've been without ham or bacon all summer!"*

"Nay, bury the pig and do without your bacon".

He dithered a while, but the lad stood there staring out him finally got to him. He killed the pig, dug a large hole, and buried it just the same as the potato.

He regretted it all night and set off in the morning to dig it up again, but when he got there somebody had built a house! Just like his house, but with its own back door, which he'd never had before.

He looked around for the green-eyed lad again, but he was nowhere to be seen. Instead he heard a buzzing sound and spotted a wasp flying around his head. He tried to swat it away, but it came closer and closer, landing on his head. He gave a jump and there he was, sitting on the bench on his allotment. He'd fallen asleep and the lad, the potato, the pig and house had all been a dream.

Potter Thompson

Once upon a time, in the town of Richmond, lived a man called Potter Thompson. He was generally a cherry soul, and well-liked by most people, but unfortunately his wife was not 'most people'. She rarely had a good or kind word to say to him, scolding him whatever he did, or didn't, do.

One evening, after a long and tiring day making pots, his wife was in a particularly bad mood. Potter was in no mood to spend any time in his own house, but instead wandered off down to the river, even considering throwing himself into the waters below the castle rather than return to his own home.

As he walked along the bank of the river, he spotted an opening in the cliffs that somehow he had never seen before, and, his wife forgotten, climbed into it. He went slowly and cautiously down the passage revealed, with the darkness slowly swallowing him, until a faint glow appeared ahead.

Turning a corner, this faint light revealed itself as a vast lamp, hung in the centre of a huge chamber. Immediately below the lamp was a stone table, with a great sword within its scabbard and a richly decorated horn.

Coming up to the table, he spotted statues lining the far side of the chamber. They looked like mighty stone warriors, lying on the floor in a row, with one wearing a simple crown of gold.

Increasingly nervous now, Potter Thompson walked closer to them and realised they were not made of stone, but were sleeping men, breathing heavily and more slowly than normal men normally do.

Nervously he returned to the table, his hands attracted remorselessly towards the sword and the horn. He put the horn around his neck and picked up the sword. As he started to draw the sword from its scabbard, the knights stirred slightly in their magical sleep. He lifted the horn to his lips, and again they stirred before he could blow.

This so terrified him, that he dropped them straight back onto the stone table and turned to run from the secret chamber. Immediately a strong wind rushed through, as though speeding him on his way, and an unearthly cry sounded around him:

> *'If thou hadst either drawn*
> *The sword or sound that horn,*
> *Thou would hadst been the luckiest man*
> *That ever was born.'*

Thus the King Arthur and his nights were allowed to fall back into their long sleep, and the day when they would rise again and come to England's aid was delayed.

Perhaps one day soon a bolder man shall find again the gloomy vault, and draw the sword and sound the horn, still laid up, and awaiting,

beneath Richmond's historic keep.

The Prophecy

There was once a rich man who lived in the West Riding of Yorkshire. One day he was riding out of town when he saw an old witch wringing her hands. She called out to the rich man and asked him to help, as her child had fallen into the dyke, but he refused to help pull the child out.

The witch was furious at this, and said to him, *"You'll have a son one day and because of this he'll die when he's twenty one."*

Well, the rich man did go onto have a son, but the witch's prophecy laid heavily on him, so he built a tower to keep his son safe. There was no door, and the window to his son's rooms was high up out of reach of the ground. His son lived in the tower with an old servant, with all his supplies sent up by a rope to his rooms.

Time passed, and the lad's twenty first birthday finally came around. It was a cold day, so they called for some more firewood to keep the tower warm. They let down the rope, and pulled up a bundle of sticks.

The lad picked up the sticks and threw them on the fire, but as he did, a snake came out of the bundle and bit him in the face, killing him quickly.

So the witches prophecy came true and she had her revenge.

The Red Cap of Close House

Close House, beside the Roman road through Addingham, is an old place, and the original homestead (now rebuilt) stood there long before the days of bluff King Hal. Formerly, when old beliefs were rife, was avowed to be under the special guardianship of an active, yet testy little hob or fairy, who went by the name of Red Cap.

A curious composite of superhuman strength and frailty was this ancient fairy. We are often told that extremes meet, and surely the proverb could not be better shown than in the singular character of this creature, who was the very type and ideal of mischief and ill-doing as well as of industrious toil.

He could play his pranks and bring disaster, as the humour swayed him, or work with might and main to his own or masters honour, the spirit of evil it might be lurking in a righteous breast, the spirit of something burning on the horizon of life, which kindled the old fire of pagan tradition and continued to live in various guises in the long after-time. There can be no doubt of his pagan forbears, being akin to the race of Kobolds who frequented favoured houses to aid the servants in their work. Here at Close House this venerable sprite had been a good little fellow in his young days, watching over flock and farm, and we were always told he had assisted in hay-time and performed sundry and other work, without any fee or reward, perchance saving an occasional cup of milk or a cosy nook by the lire-side in stormy weather. A wonderful creature truly!

But as rumour said, he one day gave the honest farm-folk the cold shoulder, and ever since has been wandering through dale and field, an idle worthless wight, no good to anyone, and tempting others, too, to idle, evil ways. Many a time have I in childhood's days, tossed the sweet mown grass in the hay-field, when tired with the rustic work have fallen down in the warm sunshine and slept. When so caught I have been teased with having seen Red Cap, though I always declared I should like to see the imp, but in sooth I never did.

Magpie rhyme (1)

One for sorrow

Two for mirth

Three for a wedding

Four for a birth

Five for a parson

Six for a clerk

Seven for a babe

Buried in the dark

The Return

There was an old fella who would come regularly into the shop for a copper's worth, and one day he dropped down dead, all of a sudden, right in the shop.

That was a bit of a bad do, to say the least, but there was worse after. Folk in the shop kept on seeing his waff (*ghost*) hovering by the counter and trade fell away to nowt.

Dealing with things like this seemed like the parson's job, so we sent for him. With the parson there, the waff appeared again, so he was challenged to depart the shop forever.

"No, no, parson", says the waff. *"I don't **want** to stay down here, but I'm not going to the Good Place until I've got my change!"*

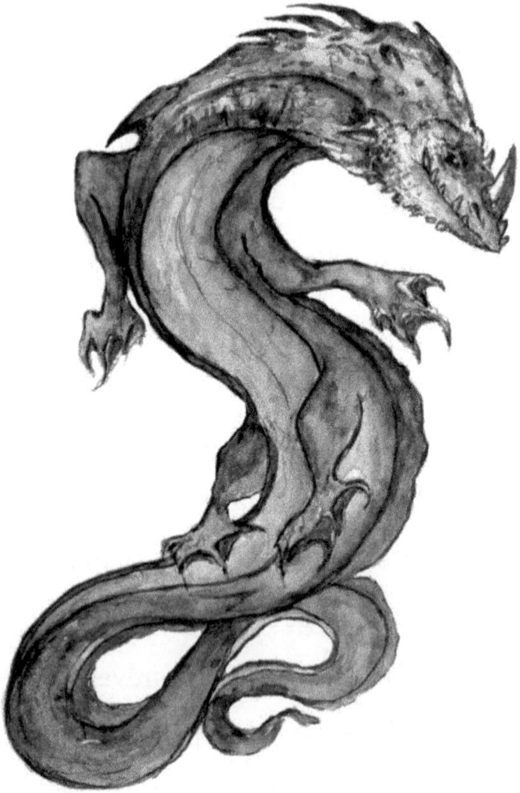

The Serpent of Handale

Handale is a quiet spot these days, set in lovely countryside, with woods and open fields set around it, but also with the coast nearby.

In ancient times, however, Handale wasn't so pleasant to live in, as these quiet woods were infested by a huge and powerful dragon, which had the power to control young women. For many years it would bring young maidens under its spell, bewitching them into leaving their homes and entering its lair, where it would feast on their youthful limbs.

A brave young man called Scaw was enraged by this waste of life, and after losing a friend to the vile worm, swore to destroy the dragon, or to perish in the attempt.

Amid the tears and prayers of his friends and family, he buckled on his armour, and made his way to the serpent's cave.

He drew his sword, and struck a rock near the entrance to announce his presence. The dragon immediately came out, blasting fire from his nostrils, and rearing high his crested head to display the poisonous sting, which had destroyed many an angry young man before.

Scaw, however, was made of braver stuff, and he held his ground. After a long and exhausting fight, the young hero prevailed, killing the dragon in the entrance to its own cave.

Clambering over the body of the beast, he found an earl's daughter still alive in the cave, whose family were so pleased with her timely rescue, they signed huge estates over to him.

The wood where he killed the dragon is called Scaw Wood to this day, and the stone coffin in which he was buried can still be found in the grounds of the old Benedictine priory nearby.

The Seven Sisters & Their Bad Neighbour

There were once seven sisters who lived together by Beldon Brook, on the edge of Lepton Great Wood. Everything they cared for on their farm thrived. Their crops grew strong and tall, their pigs grew fat on beech mast from the wood, and their fowl kept them well supplied with eggs and meat.

One of their neighbours grew jealous of their plenty. His harvest was poor compared to the sisters' and his livestock mean and scrawny. He was determined to benefit from the skill the sisters had, and sought to bind their farms together by marrying off his son to one of the sisters. After all, with seven to choose from, finding one for his son should be easy.

His son grew older, but the sisters always laughed off his son's advances. Each year, the neighbour got more frustrated with this state of affairs. His son wooed the sisters, and the sisters brushed him aside with smiles and laughter.

This carried on until one Spring when the sisters announced they intended to travel away from Lepton. They wanted to set eyes upon the wild sea in a hunt for new horizons.

Their neighbour was beside himself. He was still convinced that one day he would be able to persuade one of the sisters to marry his son, and turn around the state of his farm. By now his was convinced no one else would do. If he married his son off to anyone else, he was sure the farm would continue to get meaner and the harvest scrappier. He needed the skill and the bounty the sisters would bring with them.

With this in his heart, he set off to Yetton to see the wise woman there in the hope she would provide an answer.

*'How can I stop the sisters leaving?', h*e asked her.

'There is a way' she replied, *'but you won't like it'*.

'That's nowt to do with you, just tell me what to do'', said he.

So she gave him seven rods of poplar wood, and told him to strike each of them with a rod hard enough to draw blood, then to stick each rod into the ground and say over them the following words:

'As long as the holly grows green, here you'll be.'

Pleased with this pan, the neighbour hurried home, determined to put it into action.

He called on the sisters and pretended to be pleased they were to move away soon, following their desire for new adventures, and that he wanted to celebrate their time in Lepton before they left.

'Meet us in Lepton fields, below Th'Oggeries'' he said to them, *'we'll put a dance on at dusk so you can say goodbye to Lepton with a jig in your step'*.

The sisters, always pleased to have an excuse for dancing and merriment, came together at dusk as requested. As they crossed the fields, however, their neighbour and his sons set upon them with the poplar rods. Each sister was struck, and each rod was shoved into the ground.

As the last was planted, the neighbour said over them, *'As long as the holly grows green, here you'll be'*.

To the surprise of the neighbour, his sons, and the sisters alike, the girls were stuck fast where they stood. They stiffened and stretched towards the sky, turning wooden as the neighbour and his sons looked on.

The wise woman was not the only one with magics though, the sisters having a little of their own. Unable to stop themselves being turned into trees, they nevertheless cursed their neighbour with their last words.

'As long as the holly grows green, here we may be. But as long as we stand strong, all you grow will go wrong.'

The seven sisters still stand together in the fields above Lepton to this day, but their neighbours crops died away of blight, his livestock wasted away, the son moved far from home, and he starved before the following winter was out.

As a reminder of the wrong done to them, the ground underneath the sisters' branches will grow no crop, and animals that seek shelter there soon grow sick and waste away.

Magpie rhyme (2)

One for sorrow

Two for luck

Three for a wedding

Four for a death

Five for silver

Six for gold

Seven for a bonny lass twenty years old

Upsall and its Crocks of Gold

High up on a spur of the Hambleton Hills, overlooking the great Vale of York and the hills beyond it, and the whole country, from York into the county of Durham, stands the small village of Upsall. In this village they tell a story of a man, in days of old, found treasure near their old castle.

At the village of Upsall resided, many years ago, a man called George, who dreamed, on three nights successively, that if he went to London Bridge he would hear of something greatly to his advantage. He pondered this a while, but thought it best to take note of these dreams and set off to the capital as soon as he could.

George went, taking many days to travel the whole distance from Upsall to London on foot. Having arrived there, he waited near the centre of the bridge, until his patience was nearly exhausted, and he began to feel he had acted very foolishly indeed. A kindly Quaker, who had passed him by earlier in the day, stopped to ask why he was waiting there for so long. After some hesitation George told this kindly stranger about his dreams. The Quaker laughed at his simplicity, and told him that he had had that night a very curious dream himself, which was, that if he went and dug under an elder bush in Upsall Castle Yard, in Yorkshire, he would find a pot of gold, but he did not know where Upsall was, and inquired of the countryman if he knew?

George, reluctant to share this possible bounty, claimed he had never heard of such a place, and then, thinking his business in London was completed, returned immediately home.

As soon as he arrived in Upsall, he grabbed his spade and went to the old castle yard, without even stopping for a rest and a drink. George dug beneath the bush, and there found a pot filled with gold coins, but on the cover was an inscription in a script he did not understand.

He hid the gold in a safe place, secure he

had made his fortune, but the pot and cover were put on display in the village inn. One day, a bearded stranger came in, and while waiting for his food, saw the pot, and exclaimed with surprise!

'Why have you a pot lid, with writing in the old language?' He asked the locals. No one replied to him, so this time he asked *'Do any of you know what it says?'*.

They admitted they did not, so the stranger took the pot lid down and read it out to them:

'Look lower, where this stood
Is another twice as good'

The man of Upsall, one of the crowd, upon hearing this slipped from the inn, grabbed his space, and dashed to the old castle. This time he dug deeper below the bush, and found another pot filled with gold, far more valuable than the first.

It had taken longer to dig up the second pot than the first, and it was after dark before he managed to struggle home with his treasure. When he woke up the next morning, he emptied the gold out and noticed that this also had an inscription on the lid. It was a repeat of the first one, which he remembered had been translated as:

'Look lower, where this stood
Is another twice as good'

He went straight back to the castle, and the hole which he had not yet had time to refill. Encouraged by the inscription, he dug deeper still, and found another pot which made him rich until the end of his days.

If anyone should doubt this story, then find your way to the old castle at Upsall and you'll find the bush still there that hid the treasure beneath it. Just look for an old elder bush, near the north-west corner of the ruins.

Wadda of Mulgrave, and Bell, his Wife.

In the distance past, before the Norman invasion of these lands, a castle stood a few miles North West of Whitby, near Lythe, called Mulgrave Castle.

It stood on a hill side, but on a higher, craggier hill nearby, now stands a pile of stones known as Wadda's grave. The local people say that this is the grave of a giant, who built Mulgrave Castle.

Wadda and his wife, Bell, between them built both the old Mulgrave castle and Pickering Castle too, some twenty or so miles apart.

Wadda was said to be one of the plotters involved in the murder of Ethelred, the King of Northumberland, and needed to build himself a stronger castle. Unfortunately, Bell had already started building Pickering Castle, and they only had one hammer between them.

Rather than work on one and then the other,

they each worked alone, throwing the hammer the twenty or more miles between them. They did this with ease, just shouting beforehand, so the other was ready to catch it!

The Roman road, too, which crosses this part of the country, is named Wadda's Causeway, and was formed by the same couple for the convenience of Bell crossing the moor to milk her cow.

Wadda did the paving while his wife brought the stones in her apron. Her apron occasionally slipped, with the stones falling to the ground. Evidence of this can still be found in the area, with large heaps of stones still visible nearby.

This worthy couple had a son, also called Wadda, whose strength was equally as marvellous as that of his parents. One day, when still little more than an infant, being impatient for his mother's breast, while she was away milking her cow near Swart Hole, he seized an enormous stone, and, in a most impatient and rude manner, hurled it at her across the valley, and knocked her to the ground. She was barely hurt, yet so great was the violence with which she was struck that a considerable dent was made in the stone!

This stone remained until recent years, showing proof again of the family's great strength, though it was broken up to mend the highways not long ago.

If anyone should need further proof of the existence of these giants, look at the hill by Leland, near the site of the old castle of Mulgrave, and you will see where Wadda and Bell were buried. Two upright stones stand some twelve feet apart, marking the head and foot of the giants' grave.

A few wedding sayings:

A weddin', a woo, a clog an' a shoe
A pot full o' porride an' away they go.
(People may then pretend to take off their shoes and through them at the couple – this was known as "trashing the couple".)

Green and white
Forsaken quite.
(Green and white are unlucky colours on a wedding dress.)

The woman that changes her name
And not the first letter;
Is all for the worse
And none for the better.

Happy is the bride the sun shines on,
Blessed is the corpse the rain falls on.

Waffs at the Bridge

A waff is a ghost or wraith, sometimes appearing before death (like the bargest) as a warning.

There was a waff who was in a proper "to do". He'd forgotten where he was bound for, and why he had to go there, when he heard something grumbling and howling – it was another waff in the same pickle as him!

"*At least there's two of us then*", says the first one, and they both took heart at that, and were a little cheered.

Well, they came to a stone bridge, high over a fast and swollen river, with a force (*waterfall*) not far behind it. Hungry after some lives that river looked, and all ready and waiting for them. The waffs leaned over the wall of the bridge and looked down, spotting two chaps in an old boat they couldn't manage coming swirling down the river.

"Looks like they'll be drowned if they don't take to their oars", said waff number two.

The chaps looked up white-faced and see the two waffs looking down on them. That startled them so much they grabbed the oars, rowed like mad to the bank, and ran into the woods at a sprint.

"Eh, did you see that red haired chap?", says number one. *"He was the spitting image of you."*

"Aye", said number two. *"An the little 'un and you look alike as two pins."*

"I don't relish the thought of that", says number one. *"It's unlucky to meet a doppleganger face to face, what if they were headed up to the brig as they ran?"*

"I'm not the lad for an unlucky meeting", says number two, *"come on, lets stir ourselves!"*

And both waffs went clean out like candle flames. Just like that!

The White Horse of Wharfedale

People still regularly drown in this river, jumping over the "strid". It was said that as people drowned in the river, they would see a white horse emerging from the water, hence this poem from "Alaric Watt's Poetical Album".

O sisters, hasten we on our way,
The Wharf is wide and strong
Our father alone in his hall will say,
"My daughters linger long."
Yet, tarry awhile in the yellow moonlight,
And each shall see her own true knight,
For now in her boat of an acorn-shell
The fairy queen may be,
She dives in a water-spider's bell
To keep her revelry.
We'll drop a thistle's beard in the tide—
'Twill serve for bridles when fairies ride;
And she who shall first her White Horse see
Shall be the heiress of Bethmeslie."

Then Jeannette spoke with her eyes of light—
"O if I had fairy power,
I would change this elm to a gallant knight,
And this grey rock to a bower:
Our dwelling should be behind a screen
Of blossoming alders and laurustine;
Our hives should tempt the wild bees all,
And the swallows love our eaves,
For the eglantine should tuft our wall,
And cover their nests with leaves:
The spindle's wool should lie unspun,
And our lambs lie safe in the summer-sun,
While the merry bells ring for my knight and me,
Farewell to the halls of Bethmeslie."

Then Annot shook her golden hair–
"If I had power and will,
These rocks should change to marble rare,
And the oaks should leave the hill,
To build a dome of prouder height
Than ever yet rose in the morning light;

And every one of these slender reeds
Should be a page in green,
To lead and deck my berry-brown steeds,
And call my greyhounds in;
These lilies all should be ladies gay,
To weave the pearls for my silk array,
And none but a princely knight should see
Smiles in the lady of Bethmeslie."

Then softly said their sister May–
"I would ask neither spell nor wand;
For better I prize this white rose-spray
Plucked by my father's hand:
And little I heed the knight to see
Who seeks the heiress of Bethmeslie
Yet would I give one of these roses white
If the fairy queen would ride
Safe o'er this flood ere the dead of night,
And bear us by her side.
And then with her wing let her lift the latch
Of my father's gate, and his slumbers watch,

And touch his eyes with her glow-worm-gleams
Till he sees and blesses us in his dreams."

The night-winds howled o'er Bolton-Strid,
The flood was dark and drear,
But through it swam the Fairy-queen's steed
The lady May to bear;
And that milk-white steed was seen to skim
Like a flash of the moon on the water's brim.
The morning came, and the winds were tame,
The flood slept on the shore;
But the sisters three of Bethmeslie
Returned to its hall no more.
Now under the shade of its ruined wall
A thorn grows lonely, bare, and tall.
And there is a weak and weeping weed
Seems on its rugged stem to feed:
The shepherds sit in the green recess,
And call them Pride and Idleness,
But there is the root of a white rose-tree
Still blooms at the gate of Bethmeslie.

Woe to the maid that on morn of May

Shall see that White Horse rise !

The hope of her heart shall pass away

As the foam of his nostril flies,

Unless to her father's knee she brings

The white rose-tree's first offerings.-

There is no dew from summer-skies

Has power like the drop from a father's eyes;

And if on her cheek that tear of bliss

Shall mingle with his holy kiss,

The bloom of her cheek shall blessed be

As the Fairy's rose of Bethmeslie.

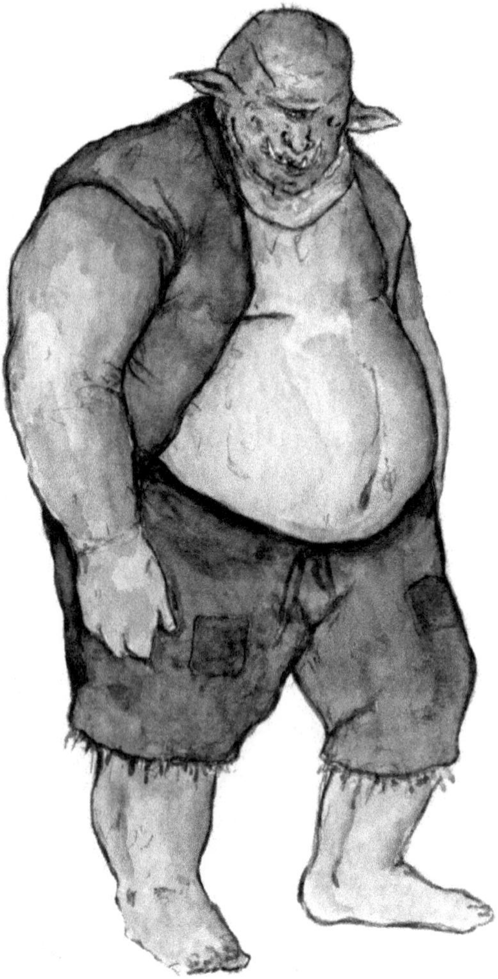

The Wicked Giant of Penhill

When the Norsemen settled in Yorkshire in the old days, they brought some of their gods too, and more importantly to this tale, some of the descendants of their gods stayed on, alive in the folk tales.

Near where Bolton Castle still stands today, and terrorising the countryside all around, lived a giant who was a descendant of Thor, the god of storms and thunder. All he cared about was his vast herd of pigs, and Wolfhead - the boarhound that he kept to help look after them. He lived in the time before the Normans came to these shores, and all were scared of him.

Every day the giant drove his swineherd through the gate of his castle on Penhill. He'd count them out and feel proud of how fat and valuable they were.

One day, walking out with his loyal boarhound Wolfhead, he saw a small flock of sheep on the hillside. *'Look at those stupid sheep'*, he said to Wolfhead. *'They are nothing compared to our great pigs, go and have some fun with them.'*

So his hound pounced on the first sheep and tore it apart. *'Another one!'* laughed the giant. So Wolfhead slaughtered one after another of the defenceless sheep, while the wicked giant laughed his socks off.

A beautiful young girl, Gunda, rushed up to him and flung herself at his feet and begged him to make his hound stop. *'Please Sir'*, she implored, *'this is my father's flock and all that he has, please call off your beast'*.

This only made the giant laugh even more, delighting in the fear she showed as another sheep was ripped to pieces in front of them. *'Perhaps I will stop him, if you make it worth my while'*, he leered at her, then grabbed her and tried to tear her clothes from her body.

She squirmed, and wriggled, and slipped from his grasp, leaving him with nothing but a small piece of cloth torn from her jacket. This made him furious, and he roared with anger while she ran away as fast as she could.

The giant, with his great heavy boots, couldn't keep up, and sent Wolfhead to catch her. She couldn't run faster than the hound, and tripped and fell in her rush to get away. As the dog jumped onto her to pin her to the ground for his master, she grabbed a rock and slammed it into the hound's nose. It howled in pain and jumped away, whining for its master. This made the giant even angrier, so he raised his club and killed the poor shepherdess on the spot.

The wicked giant had done so many evil deeds, and so terrified the locals, that he thought nothing of this terrible assault and murder, but simply returned home to his castle with his loyal hound.

A few weeks later, bringing the swine out on the morning, he noticed he was missing a young boar. He kicked his only friend, the hound Wolfhead, and ordered him to go and find the missing boar. *'Go on, you lazy old hound. Find that boar or I will whip you senseless with Thor's own belt I still wear, and leave you in the woods for the wild wolves to kill.'*

The hound wasn't happy at this treatment, and growled as followed his nose on the boar's trail. He soon found the missing boar, dead with an arrow through its heart.

The giant swore to take the hand of whoever had dared to kill his boar, and ordered his steward to make everyone within the dale who could draw a bow, come to the top of Penhill. Any man not waiting at the top of the cliff by sunset in a week's time would be thrown into the castle dungeons to rot.

In the meantime, Wolfhead had not returned. Remembering the cruel kick and the giant's words, he stayed in the forest away from his master. The giant had his men search for him, and even though they found him, he would not return when called. The giant's temper got the better of him again, and he took out his bow, and killed the only creature that had ever been his friend.

The following day, the local men were lined up waiting for him on Penhill. The giant was still angry after killing Wolfhead, and in no mood to deal gently with anyone that day. He demanded that the men assembled tell him who had shot the boar. None of them could meet his eye, and none spoke up, as they didn't know who had shot the arrow.

'You dare defy me!', the giant roared so loudly that the stones on the ground shook. *'Then out of my sight! I swear by my ancestor Thor, that I will make you speak. Tomorrow at sunset, every father shall stand*

here with his youngest child in his arms, and if you defy me again, I will show you what I am really capable of doing.'

As the men ran away, the giant was amazed to hear a quiet voice. One old man had stayed, leaning on his staff for support, and looking straight at the giant without showing a hint of fear. *'What will happen tomorrow, when the men don't give you the answer you seek?'*, asked the old man.

'I have the power of life and death over these men', the giant laughed, *'and you had better remember that and speak to me with respect'.*

'Is that your answer? If so, take heed of my words. Tomorrow is Thor's day, and if you spill one drop of blood, or cause one of the children to cry out in pain or fear, you will not enter your castle again, dead or alive', the old man warned the giant.

The wicked giant was too amazed by the actions of the old man to do much more than laugh again.

'You're just an old hermit, and you think to speak to me like that! Get back to your cave and you'll see tomorrow what I do to the likes of you'.

As the sun dipped low in the sky the following day, the local men all returned to the hillside. Slowly and sadly, they climbed the slope, each with a young child in their arms. As they got close to the top, the old hermit met them, reassuring each of them that the giant would not harm any child.

The giant watched the local men from a window in his castle, in a better mood than he'd been in for a long time. He couldn't wait to make them suffer and get a confession for the killing of his boar.

A servant interrupted him as he watched, and tried to warn him of a dream he had last night, and how the ravens and crows he could see circling the castle that day were a bad omen. The giant didn't let him finish. Angry that his pleasant fantasies of torturing the locals had been interrupted, he kicked the servant across the room and left him for dead.

This was the last straw for the long suffering servant, and struggling to his feet, he slowly and painfully dragged basket after basket of straw, wood, and peat into the main hall and set them alight.

The giant, striding out to men the local men and their children, was shocked to see nine dead boars across his path. Another nine steps and he found nine more. Every nine steps towards the meeting place this was repeated, and the giant was incandescent with rage.

As he rounded the last corner, with the peasants stood in front of him, shouted *'By the great god Thor, not only your babies, but the blood of every living soul here shall stain the hillside red tonight and the ravens shall feast themselves fat on your flesh'*.

Then he noticed the old hermit smiling at him and demanded he come and kneel in front of him immediately.

'I'm no servant of yours, if you want to speak with me, you come here. You are a braggart. Look behind you, and you shall see that I speak the truth' replied the old man.

The giant turned and saw his castle alight, with a vast cloud of smoke rising from it. He stood transfixed for a few moments, then raised his club and strode towards the hermit. Before he could strike him, however, he stopped once more, the club dropping from his hands, the colour draining from his face, and his body shook with fear.

Behind the hermit stood Gunda, the shepherdess, and Wolfhead, the hound, held back by her on a long rope. The giant stepped back further, getting close to the edge of Penhill cliff. Gunda looked at the giant, then released Wolfhead, who sprang straight at the giant's throat, the two toppling over the edge of the cliff, never to return.

A guide to West Riding Towns:

Bradford for cash

Halifax for dash

Wakefield for pride and poverty

Huddersfield for show

Sheffield what's low

Leeds for dirt and vulgarity.

The Wicked Witch of Hob's Cave

In Mulgrave woods, not far from Whitby, lived a witch called Jeannie. The whole area lived in fear of her curses and troublemaking, but few braved her home in Hob's Cave. However, one day a brave young farmer plucked up courage to go and put an end to her and her wicked ways.

He mounted his horse and rode through the woods until he arrived at Hob's Cave. He called out her name, but he hadn't even dismounted when she rushed out of her home in a fury and his courage fled just as fast. He turned his horse around and rode off as fast as he could.

The enraged witch followed, faster than his horse could gallop, and he thought his only hope would be to cross some running water before she reached him. Downhill he rode, faster than he'd ever ridden before, with Jeannie shouting the terrible punishments she'd inflict upon him once she caught up. As he looked behind him, he could see her gaining on him, just a few yards away with her wand raised over her head.

Luckily, the stream was now close by and with one last frantic effort he spurred the horse to leap from the bank into the water. Even so, the witch was so close, that as the horse splashed into the water, she brought her wand down and cut the poor animal in two. Despite that, the speed of the horse carried the farmer, still on the front part of it, safely to the far bank.

The Wise Woman of Littondale

In the 1700s, in a lonely gill not far from Arncliffe, stood a solitary cottage. A more wretched habitation the imagination cannot picture. It contained a single room, inhabited by an old woman called Bertha, who was throughout the valley accounted a wise woman, and a practiser of the "art that none may name."

In the autumn, or rather in the latter end of the summer, I set out one evening to visit the cottage of the wise woman. I had never beheld the interior, and, led on by curiosity and mischief, was determined to see it. Having arrived at the cottage, I knocked at the gate.

"*Come in*," said a voice which I knew to be Bertha's.

I entered. The old woman was seated on a three-legged stool by a peat fire, surrounded by three black cats and an old sheepdog.

*"*Well*," she exclaimed, "*what brings you here?*

What can have induced you to pay a visit to old Bertha?"

I answered, "*Be not offended. I have never before this evening viewed the interior of your cottage, and, wishing to do so, have made this visit. I wished, also, to see you perform some of your **incantations**.*"

I pronounced the last word ironically, which Bertha noticed, and said: "*Then you doubt my power, think me an impostor, and consider my incantations mere jugglery. You may think otherwise. But sit down by my humble hearth, and in less than half an hour you shall see such an instance of my power as I have never hitherto allowed mortal to witness.*"

I obeyed, and approached the fire. I now gazed around me, and minutely viewed the apartment. Three stools, an old table and a few pans, three pictures of Merlin, Nostradamus, and Michael Scott, a cauldron and a sack, with the contents of which I was unacquainted, formed the whole stock of Bertha.

The witch, having sat by me for a few minutes, rose and said, "*Now for our incantations. Behold me, but interrupt me not.*"

She then with chalk drew a circle on the floor, and in the midst of it placed a chafing dish filled with burning embers. On this she fixed the cauldron, which she had half filled with water. She then commanded me to take my station at the further end of the circle, which I did accordingly. Bertha opened the sack, and, taking from it various ingredients, threw them into the charmed pot. Amongst other articles I noticed a skeleton head, bones of different sizes, and dried carcasses of some small animals. While thus employed she continued muttering some words in an unknown language; all I remember hearing was the word *konig*. At length the water boiled, and the witch, presenting me with a glass, told me to look through it at the cauldron.

I did so and beheld a figure enveloped in the steam. At the first glance I knew not what to make of it; but I soon recognised the face of a friend and intimate acquaintance. He was dressed in his usual mode but seemed unwell and pale. I was astonished, and trembled. The figure having disappeared, Bertha removed the cauldron and extinguished the fire.

"*Now,*" said she, "*do you doubt my power? I have brought before you the form of a person who is some miles from this place, was there any deception in the appearance? I am no impostor, though you have hitherto regarded me as such.*"

She ceased speaking. I hurried to the door, and said, "*Goodnight, Bertha.*"

"*Stop,*" said she; "*I have not done with you. I will show you something more wonderful than the appearance of this evening. Tomorrow, at midnight, go and stand upon Arncliffe Bridge, and look at the water on the left side of it. Nothing will harm you; fear not.*"

"And why should I go to Arncliffe Bridge? What end can be answered by it? The place is lonely; I dread to be there at such an hour. May I have a companion?"

"No."

"Why not?"

"The charm will be broken."

'"What charm?"

"I cannot tell."

'"You will not?"

"I will not give you any further information. Obey me; nothing shall harm you."

"Well, Bertha," I said, *"you shall be obeyed. I believe you would do me no injury. I will repair to Arncliffe Bridge tomorrow at midnight. Goodnight."*

I then left the cottage and returned home. When I retired to bed I could not sleep, with restless eyes I lay ruminating upon the strange occurrences at the cottage. Morning dawned. I arose unrefreshed and fatigued. During the day I was unable to attend to my business; my coming adventure entirely engrossed my mind.

Night arrived. I repaired to the bridge. Never shall I forget the scene. It was a lovely night. The full-orbed moon was sailing peacefully through a clear blue, cloudless sky, and its beams, like streaks of silvery lustre, were dancing on the waters; and the moonlight falling on the hills formed them into a variety of fantastic shapes. Here one might behold the semblance of a ruined abbey, with towers and spires and Anglo-Saxon and Gothic arches; at another place there seemed a castle frowning in feudal grandeur, with its buttresses, battlements, and parapets. The stillness which reigned around, broken only by the murmuring of the stream, the cottages scattered here and there along its banks, and the woods wearing an autumnal tinge, all united to compose a scene of calm and perfect beauty. I leaned against the left battlement of the bridge. I waited a quarter of an hour, half an hour, an hour; nothing appeared. I listened: all was silent. I looked around: I saw nothing.

"Surely," I inwardly ejaculated, *"I have mistaken the hour? No; it must be midnight. Bertha has deceived me, fool that I am! Why have I obeyed the beldam?"*

The clock of the neighbouring church chimed; I counted the strokes — it was twelve o'clock. I had mistaken the hour, and resolved to stay a little longer on the bridge. I resumed my station, which I had quitted, and gazed on the stream. The river in that part runs in a clear, still channel, and all its music dies away. As I looked on the stream, I heard a low, moaning sound, and perceived the water violently troubled without any apparent cause.

The disturbance having continued a few minutes, ceased, and the river became calm, and again flowed on in peacefulness. What could this mean? Whence came that low, moaning sound? What caused the disturbance of the river? I asked myself these questions again and again, unable to give them any rational answer. With a slight indescribable kind of fear I bent my steps homewards.

On turning a corner of the lane that led to my father's house, a huge dog, apparently of the Newfoundland breed, crossed my path, and looked wistfully on me.

"Poor fellow!" I exclaimed, *"hast thou lost thy master? Come home with me, and I will use thee well till we find him."*

The dog followed me, and when I arrived at my place of abode I looked for it, but saw no traces of it, and I conjectured it had found its master.

On the following morning I repaired again to the cottage of the witch, and found her, as on the former occasion, seated by the fire.

"Well, Bertha," I said, *"I have obeyed you, I was yesterday, at midnight, on Arncliffe Bridge."*

"And of what sight were you a witness?"

"I saw nothing except a slight disturbance of the stream."

"I know," said she, *"that you saw a disturbance of the water; but did you behold nothing more?"*

"Nothing."

"Nothing! Your memory fails you."

"I forgot, Bertha. As I was proceeding home I met a Newfoundland dog, which I supposed belonged to some traveller."

"That dog," answered Bertha, *"never belonged to a mortal, no human being is his master. The dog you saw was a Bargest! You may perhaps have heard of him?"*

"I have frequently heard tales of Bargest, but I never credited them. If the legend of my native hills be true, a death may be expected to follow his appearance."

"You are right, and a death will follow his last night's appearance."

"Whose death?"

"Not yours."

As Bertha refused to make any further communication, I left her. In less than three hours after I left her I was informed that my friend, whose figure I had seen enveloped in the mist of the cauldron, had that morning committed suicide by drowning himself at Arncliffe Bridge, in the very spot where I beheld the disturbance of the stream.

A Yorkshire Fairy Reminiscence

A respectable female, from a village in the East Riding of Yorkshire, who is nearly related to the writer of this, beheld, when she was a little girl, a troop of fairies, "deftly footing a roundel dance" in her mother's large old parlour, even in the "garish eye of day." I have frequently heard it related by her venerable mother, and subsequently by herself. I shall give the tale as I received it from the old lady:

"My eldest daughter, Betsy, was about four years old; I remember it was on a fine summer's afternoon, or rather evening, I was seated on this chair which I now occupy; the child had been in the garden, she came into that entry or passage from the kitchen (on the right side of the entry was the old parlour door, on the left the door of the common sitting-room, the mother of the child was in a line with both the doors); the child, instead of turning towards the sitting-room, made a pause at the parlour door, which was open.

I observed her to stand, and look in very attentively; she stood several minutes, quite still. At last I saw her draw her hand quickly towards her body, she set up a loud shriek, and ran, or rather flew, to me, crying out, '*Oh, mammy, green man will heb me, green man will heb me!*' It was a long time before I could pacify her; I then asked her why she was so frightened. '*Oh, mammy*," she said, "*all t'parlour is full of addlers and menters,*' elves and fairies, I suppose she meant. She said they were dancing, and a little man in a green coat, with a gold-laced cock'd hat on his head, offered to take her hand, as if he would have her as his partner in the dance."

The mother, upon hearing this, went and looked into the old parlour, but the fairy pageant, like Prospero's spirits, had melted into thin air. Such is the account I heard of this vision of fairies: the person is still alive who witnessed, or supposed she saw it, and, though a well-informed person, still positively asserts the relation to be strictly true. I cannot say how the truth may be, I tell the tale as 'twas told to me.

Key sources & notes

A great many of the stories are straight from these sources with relatively minor changes, so there are many different "voices" and styles of story here. More recent (in copyright) sources like Gee were often a great initial source of information that I then used to track down older versions of the same story. Look out for cheap second hand copies of Gee's book, as he retold many of the tales quite nicely.

Some things have different spellings in different stories, for example Barguest and Bargest – I kept the spelling I found in the original of each to make it easier if anyone wants to search for variation of the stories.

The key exceptions are 'The Seven Sisters and their Bad Neighbour', and the 'Golden Cradle and Castle Hill', which are my attempt at taking tiny scraps of legend (e.g., 'Legends say there is a golden cradle on Castle Hill in Huddersfield', or 'those trees used to be witches') and tying them into a fuller story. There were also the occasional tales directly from a source such as a newspaper – I've tended to put the reference to them at the start of the text.

Throughout the lot, I've been cheeky at times and replaced the occasional name with that of one of my children, Jennifer and George, or where wasn't really location specific, I've dropped in Huddersfield place names. Some could also be wider English (or European) folk tales, but where a source like Gee or Parkinson has claimed it for Yorkshire, I've followed suit!

References

Briggs, K. (1970 / 71). *A dictionary of British folktales in the English language. Incorporating the F.J. Norton collection.* London: Routledge.
A 3 volume set, comprehensively covering British folktales. A massive collection.

Crossland, J. (1931). *Legends and folklore of Yorkshire.* London: Collins.
Nice collection of Yorkshire tales. The book isn't actually dated, but the preface says 1931!

Dixon, J. (c. 1881). *Chronicles and stories of the Craven dales.* London: Simpkin, Marshall & co.
A mass of detail about the Craven area, including local folklore and tales.

Gee, H. (1952). *Folk tales of Yorkshire.* London: Thomas Nelson & Sons.
Brilliant retelling of Yorkshire tales, in a compact hardback book. Often available cheaply second-hand!

Halliday, W. & Umpleby, A. (1949). *The White Rose Garland of Yorkshire Dialect Verse of Local and Folk-Lore Rhymes.* London: Dent and Sons.
This pulled together a great deal of dialect verse and folklore from across the centuries.

Henderson, W. (1879). *Notes on the folk-lore of the Northern counties of England and the Borders.* London: Satchell, Peyton & Co.
Wider than just Yorkshire, this collection was published for the Folklore Society and is a massive collection of lore and stories.

Horfall Turner, J. (Ed.) (1888/1890). *Yorkshire notes and queries, with which is incorporated Yorkshire folk-lore journal.*
A strange and fascinating journal containing everything from births and deaths in the area to extended details about prominent buildings. The Yorkshire folk-lore journal sections have a mix of lore, stories, and people asking about local traditions.

Logan, W. (1869). *A pedlar's pack of ballads and songs. With illustrative notes.* Edinburgh: Patterson. *Freely available online, collection of ballads and songs from across the UK.*

Moorman, F. (1920) *Tales of the Ridings* and *More Tales of the Ridings.* London: Elkin Mathews. *These two books have tales about the Yorkshire Ridings and characters within them. They also include a few folktales.*

Parkinson, T. (1888). *Yorkshire Legends and Traditions.* London: Elliot Stock. *Freely available online, a fairly comprehensive collection of Yorkshire tales. A brilliant source of these sort of things!*

Tongue, R. (1970). *Forgotten folk-tales of the English Counties.* London: Routledge. *Ruth Tongue managed to collect many tales, and fragments of tales, that you might not find elsewhere.*

The beggars' and vagrants' litany

From Hell, Hull, and Halifax, good Lord deliver us.

(At Hull, vagrants found begging in the streets were whipped and set in the stocks. In Halifax, anyone found stealing cloth was instantly, without trial, beheaded with an execution machine called a "maiden".)

Lightning Source UK Ltd.
Milton Keynes UK
UKHW020735161222
414034UK00019B/1704